The Spirit and the Flesh

The Spirit and the Flesh

by TJ Dias

Matador
9 Priory Business Park,
Wistow Road, Kibworth Beauchamp,
Leicestershire. LE8 0RX
Tel: 0116 279 2299
Email: books@troubador.co.uk
Web: www.troubador.co.uk/matador
Twitter: @matadorbooks

ISBN 978 1789018 141

British Library Cataloguing in Publication Data.
A catalogue record for this book is available from the British Library.

Printed and bound in Great Britain by 4edge Limited
Typeset in 12pt Adobe Garamond Pro by Troubador Publishing Ltd, Leicester, UK

Matador is an imprint of Troubador Publishing Ltd

Acknowledgments

First and foremost, I thank Almighty God for the successful completion and publication of this work.

Thanks to the Blessed Mother, St Joseph, St Anthony of Padua, St Francis de Sales, St Therese of Lisieux, Hilaire Belloc and G.K. Chesterton for all being at my side on this endeavour.

Finally, thanks to my dad for his help and support.

1

That Catholic Killjoy!

'Boy oh boy, Amsterdam's gonna be great!' said Roger to Paul after swilling down some of his pint of lager. 'My mouth is positively watering for it. I can't wait!'

Paul smiled and nodded in agreement.

'I reckon Amsterdam better stock right up on its beer and import more weed before I come into town,' Roger added. 'I'm gonna be living it up like there's no tomorrow.'

Paul chuckled before adding his intentions.

'You can count me in with living it up like there's no tomorrow,' he said excitedly. 'This'll be my first-ever time in Amsterdam, so nothing's gonna stop me exploring everything the place has to offer.'

Paul Thompson and Roger Swindon were housemates and undergraduate law students at Warwick University. They were supping beer at their student union bar and excitedly looking forward to an upcoming weekend break in Holland's capital city, leaving on Friday morning and coming back Sunday afternoon. They'd be going with their new housemate, Sean Brady, who presently wasn't with them.

'I keep forgetting this'll be your first time in Amsterdam,' Roger said to Paul. 'You're in for the ride of your life, mate. I'll show you all the best places: the best shops; the best clubs; where to drink the best beer; where to smoke the best joints; and where to find the best-looking ladies of the night. Yeah, this weekend is gonna be a fiesta of blissful, unconstrained, uninhibited, no-holds-barred pleasure-seeking.'

'Sounds good to me,' said Paul, licking his lips.

'I remember my first-ever time in Amsterdam,' Roger began to recollect. 'When I was shown around De Wallen – the red-light district – for the very first time… it just absolutely blew me away. Then when I saw the ladies of the night for the first time, I almost collapsed with excitement.'

An excited gleam came into Paul's eyes at Roger's words.

'What are the ladies of the night like?' he asked. 'I mean, are there many pretty ones?'

'There certainly are,' replied Roger. 'Obviously there's a few ugly ones, as well as a few fat ones and a few old ones. You'll see when you're there. You get a variety. There's blondes, brunettes, black women, Asian women, Latinos, Filipinos. There's always a good selection on offer to cater for everyone's tastes. Personally, I'm partial to a Dutch blonde, but I'm sure you'll find one that tickles your own particular fancy.'

Paul hunched his shoulders before taking a sip of his lager.

'I'm not sure I've got the nerve to actually pay a visit to one of them,' he admitted.

Roger screwed up his face.

'What are you, a man or a mouse?' he scowled. 'I thought you just said you were ready to explore everything the town has to offer?'

Paul remained silent. Though he wouldn't admit it, the idea of visiting a prostitute made him apprehensive. It crossed his line a little.

'I dunno,' said Roger, shaking his head. 'You disappoint me, Paul. I had you down as a liberal-minded type of man without any hang-ups or reservations about indulging in life's pleasures.'

'I am liberal-minded!' Paul insisted. 'But I'll see how I feel about it when I'm there. Are you definitely going to visit one?'

'You're damn right I am,' Roger replied, emphatically. 'It's the main reason I'm going.'

Paul laughed.

'One lucky lady, whoever it may be, will be granted access to my Greek god body,' said Roger, alluding to his bulky, power-lifter's physique that was formed during frequent visits to the gym.

'I've got absolutely no hesitation about it,' he continued. 'As far as I'm concerned, there'll be no limits to my search for pleasure on this holiday. We've only got one life and we have to live for the here and now. We should never allow potential moments of pleasure to pass us by. Satisfying our appetites is what life is all about and I'm sorry for anyone who doesn't believe that.'

Roger then felt the need to throw an accusation at Paul.

'I reckon you're spending too much time with that holier-than-thou monk now living with us. His influence is rubbing off on you, inhibiting you and making you fearful.'

'You talking about Sean?' asked Paul.

'Yeah,' said Roger. 'I don't want to be horrible, but I really don't know why he's coming to Amsterdam with us. I've got this fear he's gonna stifle our fun out there.'

Up till now, Roger had kept his feelings about Sean to himself, but drink was finally bringing out his inner concerns.

'I mean, what's he gonna be doing?' Roger continued. 'He doesn't drink, he doesn't smoke, he's clearly not into erotic entertainment. He's made it clear he'll be keeping away from the red-light district. So what's the point of him coming?'

'Well, I've never been, but there must be more to Amsterdam than just the red-light district,' Paul proposed.

'Really?' answered Roger. 'I suppose you're only going to Amsterdam for the tulips, aren't you?'

Paul shook his head.

'I'm going for the same things as you,' he said. 'But Sean's different to us. He has different morals. You've got to respect that.'

'I do respect that,' claimed Roger. 'I'm just wondering why someone with his kind of morals wants to join us on what's supposed to be a trip of unrestricted pleasure. That's what this trip is gonna be all about. So why is he joining us?'

'Because we asked him,' Paul reminded Roger.

'We asked him out of courtesy,' said Roger, 'because he's our new housemate. But we didn't think he'd say "yes", did we? What gets me is that he hasn't come to any pubs or clubs with us, or socialised with us very much. When he does go out, it's usually with his church friends, so I don't know why he agreed to join us on this trip. I mean, are we gonna be able to do all the stuff we wanna to do with him tagging along?'

'He won't get in the way of our enjoyment,' Paul asserted. 'When we go to the red-light district, he's gonna go his own separate way. He won't interfere with us.'

The man in question, Sean Brady, was a post-graduate theology student who had strong religious convictions. In fact, he was a staunch Roman Catholic in the traditionalist, orthodox mould. Whereas Roger and Paul were on the same course and had shared a house for almost a year, Sean had only come into their lives in the past six weeks, when their landlord advertised for a third lodger. He was the only one they could find who was prepared to live in their scruffy, unkept, semi-detached house.

'You're really not that keen on Sean, are you?' Paul accused Roger.

'I've got nothing against him,' Roger replied, defensively. 'But there are just things about him that really get to me.'

'Like what?' asked Paul.

'Like the fact that he seems to lead such an unexciting, mundane life,' Roger bluntly replied. 'He's obviously ended up all repressed and inhibited by that religion of his, which was no doubt brainwashed into him since he was a baby. It's religion that's made him the bland, unexciting person he is. And he's such a straight-laced, clean-cut goody-two-shoes. Doesn't he get on your nerves just a little bit?'

Paul shook his head.

'I think he's alright,' he replied. 'He's actually a really nice person when you get to know him. But you've not tried to get to know him.'

'Just because he shares the rent with us doesn't mean I have to go out of my way to be friends with him,' said Roger. 'And anyway, you say I've not tried to get to know him but he's the one who stays out of our living room every evening and keeps to his own room. He's the unsociable one.'

'He stays out of the living room to avoid the things we watch on TV,' said Paul, 'a lot of which he finds immoral.'

'Immoral?' queried Roger. 'But he won't even watch soap operas or family-friendly sitcoms with us. Isn't that a bit extreme?'

'It seems a bit extreme to us,' said Paul, 'but he obviously finds those programmes not to his liking. Like I said, you've got to respect his morals.'

'His morals went out in the Victorian age,' quipped Roger. 'We're living in the year 2001, not 1901, and yet his morals are more old-fashioned than my grandparents'. I'm not kidding. At twenty-three he's more of an old fuddy-duddy than my granddad, who's in his eighties! And I don't know what he does alone in his room most evenings. Life must be such a drag for him. You know him better than I do. What does he do with himself?'

'I know he prays a lot,' Paul informed Roger, 'and he reads and studies. He's very knowledgeable, and he's actually quite interesting to listen to. He's really intelligent.'

'A Jesus freak that's really intelligent?' Roger jibed. 'Are you sure there's such a thing? I mean, to believe in Christianity or any other religion you really have to have checked your brains in. I'm so glad I wasn't brought up in a religious household and brainwashed into all that nonsense.'

'You know, I was brought up in the Catholic faith,' Paul reminded Roger.

'I know,' said Roger, 'but at least you had the sense to reject it and see it for the superstitious nonsense that it is. You grew up and grew out of it. Sean didn't.'

'What makes you so sure it's all superstitious nonsense?' asked Paul.

Roger briefly stared at Paul with an open mouth.

'Are you a believer, then?' he asked.

Paul had a brief think before replying.

'I'm not really a believer, but I wouldn't completely dismiss it. I like to keep an open mind on things.'

'Huh,' Roger groaned. 'Y'know, these Christians believe in all their nonsense because they *want* to believe it. It's all wishful thinking. They have little or no rational evidence to support their beliefs.'

With that bold statement Roger swilled down more of his pint.

'I wouldn't be too sure they don't have any evidence,' Paul responded. 'Sean has some evidence. He believes he was miraculously healed after he had that car accident. You know about his accident five years ago? You can still see the scarring on the side of his head.'

'Yes, I know about his accident and I've noticed his scarring,' Roger acknowledged. 'I guarantee you he wasn't miraculously healed. He just happened to make an unusually fast recovery after being badly hurt. These things happen occasionally.'

'But he wasn't just badly hurt,' Paul pointed out, 'he was all set to be pronounced dead. The medics gave him no chance. Then he miraculously recovered. Not only that, he made a full recovery. The story even made the local news up in Newcastle where he's from.'

'And you believe his recovery was a miracle?' scoffed Roger.

Paul had a brief think.

'Well… it might have been,' he eventually said with eyes full of hope.

Roger smiled wryly while shaking his head.

'How gullible can you get?' he said. 'Y'know, I bet Sean'll try to preach to us while we're on this trip because of you. He knows you're open to his religious hogwash. A couple of times he's tried to evangelise and push his religion on me, but I wouldn't stand for it – I just treated him with contempt and he stopped. But I bet while we're in Amsterdam he'll preach to us and try to warn us of the wicked sins we'll be committing, and no doubt he'll be telling us about the hellfire and damnation that will come our way.'

'He's not gonna preach to us,' Paul responded. 'He's not like that. What we get up to in the red-light district is our own business; he knows that.'

'I wouldn't bet on it,' Roger asserted. 'I'm telling you, there's a hidden reason why he's joining us on this trip. I'm sure he's got it in his mind to somehow discourage us and make us feel guilty and uncomfortable about what we'll be doing.'

Roger finished the remainder of his pint.

'Then again,' he continued, 'on second thoughts, I hope he does try to preach to us. It'll give me a chance to get back at him. If he wants an argument or a debate I'll more than give him one. And as I've got designs on being the best lawyer in Britain I'll enjoy arguing things out with him and coming out on top. With only plain, rational argument I'll destroy his mad beliefs once and for all. If he dares to preach to us I'll be totally ruthless in my retaliation, and I won't be showing him any sensitivity.'

'He's very knowledgeable and well read,' said Paul. 'I'm sure he'll give you a run for your money in a debate.'

'D'you reckon?' a defiant Roger retorted. 'Well, we'll see about that.'

2

A Ray of Orthodoxy in a Modern World

While Roger and Paul were downing pints at the student pub, their housemate Sean was back at the house. He was in his room, sitting in his armchair, relaxing and listening to some calming classical music on his CD player. With closed eyes he was locked in deep thought over the trip to Amsterdam. He knew full well that Roger and Paul had only asked him to join them on this trip out of courtesy. He also knew they'd expected him to turn them down… which to their alarm he didn't! He had his reasons for agreeing to join them.

Sean Brady was a Geordie of Irish heritage, born and bred in Newcastle. He was a graduate from Leeds Trinity College and was now embarking on a master's degree in theology at Warwick. His long-term goal was to become both a writer and an apologist for the Catholic faith. And whereas he was deeply religious, his two housemates were most certainly not; they just weren't on his wavelength. So, in the six weeks he'd spent living with Roger and Paul he'd struggled to fit in, though he found Paul the easier one to communicate with. He found Roger too headstrong, too self-righteous, with too much of a forceful, overbearing personality to go with his bulky power-lifter's physique. But Sean acknowledged that, along with the muscles, Roger was blessed with an intellect – even if it was a little misguided.

In the short time he'd been living with them, Sean had come to view both Roger and Paul as typical products of the modern world, especially Roger. They seemed to have little interest in matters of the eternal and were only interested in the here and now, the present moment, seeing earthly pleasures as the main reason for living. With these two for housemates he felt very much the odd man out. But then again, as a traditional, orthodox Roman Catholic, he felt out of place in the modern world in general. For example, he believed in the existence of absolute truth and absolute morality – the very two things that most of modern society rejected. He also believed in the existence of a natural moral law and a natural order ordained by God, and this natural law and natural order was fixed and permanent. He believed anything inherently good remained good, and time could never change what was inherently good. Likewise, anything inherently evil would always remain evil, and time could never change what was inherently evil. For Sean, the idea that truth and morality could "change with the times" was the great Satanic lie that was sweeping the modern world and corrupting it.

Sean felt absolutely no inclination to get with the times. He was firm and unswerving in his principles. He stood firm in his morals, not worrying about what the rest of the world might think of him, or whether the rest of the world might mock him and laugh at him. He refused to cave in to human respect.

But whilst Sean was now very steadfast in his beliefs, his religious convictions hadn't always been so strong. He was brought up in a household with a very devout Catholic mother but a father who was indifferent, and in his teenage years Sean followed in his dad's footsteps for a time, straying from the faith and becoming agnostic. He got involved with quite a riotous group of lads, who drank heavily, smoked and were into pornography, and their influence rubbed off on him. His loss of faith was also brought on by a developed interest in philosophy – especially the secular, atheistic sort – which made him question everything, including the faith he was brought up with. In the midst of this, he changed into somewhat of an "anything goes" liberal, becoming a heavy drinker and a smoker. However, his mother never stopped praying for him to come back to his faith.

Sean lost his faith but found it again in the aftermath of an event that would change his life forever. The event was a serious car accident which in normal circumstances should have ended his life. The accident occurred when Sean went for a "fun" drive with one of his pals, who was driving. Both he and his friend had had a fair bit to drink before this fun drive, resulting in his friend recklessly turning too sharply into a side street and catching the kerb, which caused the car to flip over. While Sean's friend somehow managed to escape serious injury by clinging to the steering wheel, Sean was knocked unconscious and fell into a coma. By the time the ambulance reached the hospital the medics feared the worst. His family were told he almost certainly wouldn't make it. But despite doctors giving him no chance, his family still prayed unceasingly for him, including his religiously lapsed dad. And it seemed their prayers were answered. Against all the odds, Sean survived. Not only that but his condition stabilised.

Despite his seemingly miraculous return from the dead, doctors were sure that Sean would have severe neurological problems for the remainder of his life. An MRI brain scan backed up this prognosis. However, it seemed the miracles weren't over yet. His family continued to pray incessantly for him and gave him holy water from Lourdes to drink, and within a few weeks of the accident Sean had made unexpected progress. Doctors discovered, to their befuddlement, that his condition was actually reversing itself. Within three months he'd fully recovered from his head injuries, save for some scarring. New brain scans showed he was back to normal, leaving his doctors perplexed and dumbfounded.

In the aftermath of these extraordinary events, Sean gave his life back to Christ and returned to his Catholic faith. His healing – which he was sure was a miraculous gift from Christ – gave him a strength of faith he'd never had before. Indeed, it had the effect of giving him an almost unshakeable faith.

Because drink was partly responsible for the accident, Sean felt the need to completely abstain from alcohol, and he pledged himself to a life of temperance. It also dawned on him that before he became a drinker and smoker (and when his faith was still strong) he was a much happier and more content person.

In the midst of Sean coming back to his faith, he came to appreciate that many in the world were without faith. Even his home city of Newcastle – a city which had historically always had a strong Catholic presence (due to Irish immigration) – was now, in 2001, secularised and indifferent to Christian morals, like the rest of Britain. Secularists – composed of liberals, Marxists, humanists and other atheistic groups – were well and truly in control of the world around him. And he came to understand that this move away from Christian morals hadn't taken place by accident – there was a group of people in the world who had accumulated great political and economic power, and this group had deliberately set out to put an end to the Christian influence on the world and establish a "new world order", putting Man at the centre of all things, as opposed to God or Christ.

Sean saw several negative aspects to a society turning its back on Christ, but three major consequences in particular.

The first was the loss of a sense of sin, with people believing they could do exactly as they pleased without fear of the consequences of breaking God's laws. Following on from this was the rejection of the idea that man is cursed by original sin (passed on by Adam and Eve), that he is a fallen creature in need of a Saviour, in need of being spiritually brought back to life by a divine Redeemer.

The second was the lack of appreciation of the existence of eternity or an afterlife, prompting people to only live for the present moment – so people's lives become driven by the search for earthly pleasure and comforts, neglecting the spirit of sacrifice or selflessness. Along with this, there was no longer an appreciation of the existence of heaven or hell and little or no concept that a person's behaviour and choices they made on earth would have a bearing on their eternal destiny – either heaven or hell forever!

The third major consequence he saw, of the emergence of atheism and the rejection of Christ, was the rejection of absolute truth and absolute morals, so all morality becomes relative – in other words, there were no longer any absolute standards of right and wrong. This moral relativism led to a breakdown of sexual ethics, and, in turn, sexual immorality had a detrimental effect on the institutions of marriage and family. With marriage and family being the pillars that a strong society is built upon, when these institutions become weakened, society will automatically weaken with it.

Sean came to understand that in a culture where there are no absolute standards of right and wrong, people will always be drawn towards living according to feelings and impulses, to whatever pleases the senses and feels good, as opposed to what is actually good. The inevitable end result is a culture of self-gratification, naturally leaning towards selfishness. In a culture such as this, vice will always have dominion over virtue – and the flesh will always have dominion over the spirit. But as far as Sean was concerned, living by the philosophy of moral relativism and "doing what thou wilt" – in defiance of God's natural moral law – could never lead to happiness. It would always lead to the very opposite, because rebellion against the natural law kills the life of grace in the soul and leads to spiritual darkness, therefore depriving a person of any true lasting joy and ultimately leading that person to hell.

For Sean, nothing could better embody the culture of self-gratification than the red-light district of Amsterdam – often described as the "liberal man's paradise" and the "realm of no limits" – where, theoretically, a man could fulfil all his earthly wants and desires. Sean's housemates, Roger and Paul, had fallen for this proposition, and this was the bait that was luring them to Amsterdam. However, the reason Sean had agreed to join them on this trip – as Roger rightly suspected – was to throw a spanner in their works. It was his intention to discourage Roger and Paul with words, to give them something to think about. He believed that they were both on the road to hell, and it was his moral duty to do all he could to lead them out of their current darkness, through lots of prayer and penance, and through evangelising to them in as effective a way as he knew how.

Sean was ready for an argument. He was bracing himself for the inevitable attacks that would come from Roger for not joining in with all the fun and frolics. From the day they first met there'd been a tension between himself and Roger; they'd struggled to get on friendly terms with one another due to nothing more than a clash of personalities and clash of outlooks. But Sean knew there had to be a showdown between them, where they could settle their differences in a "friendly" argument. Sean was eager to get things off his chest to Roger, and he'd set his sights on this upcoming weekend break in

Amsterdam to have a lot of serious conversation and debate with him.

In the event of them having an intellectual debate, Sean was bright enough to know that he'd have to meet Roger on his wavelength by keeping supernatural propositions in reserve and basing his arguments more on reason and logic. He was prepared to show that his religious and moral convictions were based on reason and logic and not just on blind faith. And by God's grace he was ready to give answers and repel any attacks from his sceptical housemate with nothing less than what he held to be the truth.

3

Brits Abroad

The first day of their three-day Dutch adventure had arrived. It was a bright, warmish Friday afternoon in the centre of Amsterdam. After their flight from Heathrow, and then train journey from Schiphol airport to Amsterdam Centraal station, Roger, Paul and Sean were now walking the streets of Holland's capital city – this after checking in to their hotel (which happily for Roger was situated halfway between the station and the red-light district). They were walking along the Damrak – which could be described as central Amsterdam's "high street". They'd decided to head out and get a bite to eat, and as they walked they took in the sights, sounds and atmosphere of central Amsterdam, absorbing the city's ambience.

The Renaissance architecture, canals and fast-moving trams on the spacious, hectic roads made immediate impressions on Paul and Sean, who'd never been before, and they were both stirred by the city's picturesque charm. And all three of them experienced the usual excitement and adrenalin rush of being in a foreign land, of being somewhere different.

Amsterdam was a city that built its name on trade and commerce. A major modern-day trade of Amsterdam's was the tourist industry, and there was no shortage of tourists about, especially British ones.

In the midst of this touristy atmosphere, Roger, Paul and Sean ambled around to find somewhere where they could eat. Eventually they found a food van selling Dutch hotdogs (*knackwursts*). They all had one each. After eating these they moved on and soon came across another food van, this time selling *stroopwafels* – disc-shaped biscuits made with compressed wafers and syrup – and they bought and happily devoured a batch of these.

After eating, they walked about a bit more. Roger pointed out to Paul and Sean central Amsterdam's most famous monuments, but he was keen to get all this mundane sightseeing stuff out of the way as quickly as possible so he could head towards the red-light area. Meanwhile, Sean was keen to visit the Basilica of St Nicholas, Amsterdam's largest Catholic place of worship (he planned to go there for Sunday Mass), but he reasoned that Roger wouldn't be keen to walk near any church, so he decided to save it for later when he was on his own.

Eventually, Roger took Paul and Sean along the Damrak to the start of a side street which led to the district of De Wallen – the red-light district. Roger pointed in the direction of the infamous area and spoke.

'There it is,' he said, excitedly. 'Heaven is a place on earth – and that's where you'll find it!'

Paul looked on with a gleam in his eyes. He was filled with curiosity.

Roger then turned to Sean.

'Are you sure you won't be joining us there later?' he asked him.

Sean fervidly shook his head.

Roger and Paul then began to engage in their own conversation. As they talked, Sean's attention was drawn to a young busker sitting to the left of him at the start of the side street where they were standing. The busker was sitting on some flattened cardboard, strumming an acoustic guitar without singing. Sean was compelled to walk over to him, which he did. After approaching the busker, he exchanged some friendly words with him and discovered he was English, and then he generously handed him a couple of gilders.

'Thank you, sir,' the friendly-faced English busker said. 'Have a nice day and God bless you.'

There was genuine warmth and kindness in the English busker's voice, which impressed Sean – who would gladly have handed him a couple of gilders more. Sean then walked back to Roger and Paul and was greeted by a look of appreciation from Paul, who was impressed by the display of generosity.

After a little more walking around, they decided to embark on that very British custom – a pub crawl. Roger guided them to a British pub he knew well, just on the outskirts of the red-light district. The pub was called The Saint George, and a large St George flag was displayed on the outside canopy (Amsterdam had quite a smattering of British and Irish pubs, to cater for the hordes of tourists which flooded in from these isles). Inside, the pub was decked out like a typical traditional British pub. In the background could be heard a jukebox playing some Britpop music. And to go with this very British setting was a strong British presence. The air was thick with the sound of various British dialects. For added authenticity, The Saint George served traditional British beers and food, and a barman and two barmaids all wearing St George flag T-shirts were serving at the bar.

In the crowded pub, Roger and Paul ordered pints of lager, whilst teetotaller Sean made do with a mineral water. They managed to find a table for themselves and sat down with their drinks.

'It feels like we're still in England,' said Paul. 'I can't believe how many Brits are here. There's tons of us.'

'I told you,' said Roger. 'We always outnumber the natives when you get near the red-light area.'

While Roger and Paul continued to chat, a quiet Sean was busy observing his surroundings. It felt odd being in a foreign land and yet finding himself in such a familiar setting. Then he turned his attention to Roger, who was proposing to Paul his plans for the day.

'We'll go to a couple more pubs after this, then I'll show you around the red light,' he told him. 'I've got our programme all mapped out. We'll visit some X-rated shops, then I'll take you to a coffee shop to smoke a joint or two, then we'll visit another pub for more beer. And we can repeat that cycle as often as you want. How's that for a plan?'

'Yeah, I'm game for that,' said a smiling Paul. 'You lead and I'll follow.'

'Of course, the red light doesn't really come alive until after dark,' said Roger. 'That's when the ladies of the night come on display! I'll be carefully examining every single brothel window until I've found the very best-looking babe to splash my cash on. After that we'll end the night at an erotic club where we can watch a live sex show – that's not a bad way to end a Friday night, eh?'

Roger glanced at Sean as he spoke. He enjoyed shocking him. Meanwhile, shivers of excitement ran through Paul, who was more than game for Roger's proposals for the night. Roger then turned to Sean.

'So, what will you be doing today?' he asked. 'I mean, seeing as you won't be joining us in the red-light area, how will you be spending your time?'

'I'll just wander around and take in some more of the atmosphere and scenery,' Sean replied in his pleasant Geordie accent. 'Then I might go back to the hotel and just relax for a bit before coming out again.'

Roger rolled his eyes, still unsure why Sean had joined them on the trip.

Paul then had a suggestion for Roger.

'What say we meet up later with Sean for supper at a restaurant?'

Roger paused before responding.

'Yeah… we could do,' he eventually said, pretending to be keen on the idea – but really he preferred Sean to be out of the way.

Time passed, and the pub remained busy, full of tourists – mostly groups of British lads. There were lots of shouts and laughter, lots of profanities and four-letter words, and no shortage of rowdiness. Roger began to take notice of one of the barmaids busily serving behind the bar. She was a youngish, pretty redhead, and he wasn't the only man in the pub whose attention she'd managed to attract.

'Check out the redhead at the bar,' Roger told Paul and Sean. 'Not bad, eh? I'm not normally into redheads but I wouldn't say no to her. Y'know, if we find someone as good-looking as that in the brothel windows tonight I'll be well pleased. She's an absolute doll. She's just about worthy of me.'

Paul let out a loud laugh at Roger's arrogance.

As Roger was in the barmaid's line of sight, he pumped out his chest muscles in an effort to impress her with his physique, but he was slightly annoyed that she seemed to focus more attention on Sean. Sean was tall, slender and blessed with Irish good looks (despite the scarring on the side of his head, he always managed to attract attention from females).

Roger then proceeded to come out with a string of lewd, lustful comments over the barmaid, not worrying about offending Sean with his language. He actually wanted to draw Sean into an argument, into a discussion where they could put their differing worldviews up against one another. He also wanted an argument that would give him an opportunity to dismantle Sean's religious beliefs. Meanwhile, Sean wanted to gently rebuke Roger for his crass comments but was stuck for the right words.

'Yeah, Amsterdam was made for us British,' Roger began to assert. 'Once we Brits get a sniff of drink, drugs and depravity, there's no holding us back. We're like rampant, unstoppable rhinos when it comes to enjoying the pleasurable things in life – it's in our genes.'

Sean put on a forced smile at Roger's words, and again didn't comment. He wanted to respond but was worried that if he sounded too preachy it could make Roger worse. He knew his words had to be right.

'No one can party or let loose like us British,' Roger continued. 'If there was a competition to find the world's greatest party animals, we'd win it. We know what life's all about. Drink, drugs and depravity! That's what life's all about. Ha, ha, ha!'

Roger took a swig of his pint before continuing.

'I wonder if I'm gonna get the same old attention from the ladies when we explore the brothel windows tonight. I don't wanna brag or boast, but whenever I visit they always seem to fix their eyes on me. I suppose it must be my looks and muscles that attract them.'

As he spoke, Roger flexed his chest muscles under his shirt. He then had more to say.

'I remember last year when I was in Amsterdam, this great fat Filipino lady actually came out of her brothel to try and coax me in. I wanted to say, "You should be paying me, dear!" Ha, ha, ha!'

For the rest of their stay in the pub, Roger came out with lots of graphic, vulgar talk revolving around his past experiences in Amsterdam and what he planned to do on this visit. As usual, he was deliberately profane with his language as he got a kick out of offending Sean. He enjoyed being a figure of contrast to the theologian's piety and clean ways. As for Sean, the whole point of him coming to Amsterdam was to challenge Roger and Paul's liberal outlook and give them something to think about; unfortunately, he found himself stuck for the right words.

4

The Origin of Man

After their drink at The Saint George, the three of them made their way over to Molly Malone's – a large, traditional Irish pub, again very close to the red-light district. This was a favourite pub of Roger's. As in The Saint George, this pub seemed to be packed with tourists, mainly Brits, though again they managed to find a table for themselves. Traditional Irish music could be heard above the noise, and the pub served authentic Irish stout imported from Dublin – of which Roger and Paul had a pint each.

'What say after this pint we head right into the red light?' Roger asked Paul. 'I'll show you all the lovely delights it has to offer.'

'I'm game for that,' Paul replied, excitedly.

'I'm gonna take you to the world's greatest playground for adults,' said Roger. 'There's no better place on earth for a man to satisfy his natural, primal, animalistic urges; urges we *all* have.'

Sean now felt he had to challenge Roger's provocative words. As discreetly as possible, he bowed his head in silent prayer, asking for both the courage and the words to say something back.

'Everyone has urges and impulses that need satisfying,' Roger continued, 'even people who call themselves Christian. And this is *the* city where a man can satisfy them!'

'Well, I certainly intend to satisfy them while I'm here,' said Paul.

'A man can only be truly happy when he is liberated from the shackles that "civilised" society puts upon him,' Roger put forward. 'We can only be happy when we break free from all the social rules and boundaries placed upon us and allow our natural animal instincts a free reign. This is what truly liberates us.'

Suddenly, Sean mustered up the courage to speak.

'Freedom and liberty come from knowing truth,' he said, boldly. 'Freedom and liberty together is a state of mind that can only come when one lives in the truth.'

At last Sean had found the nerve to say something to Roger, and Roger was actually glad that Sean had finally responded to him because this paved the way for a good verbal duel between them to finally begin.

'Also, a person who chooses to respect rules and boundaries exercises his freedom just as much as a person who chooses not to,' Sean then added.

Roger swilled a little of his pint before coming back at Sean.

'Freedom and liberty come to us when we're allowed to put aside the social constraints that keep our true natural instincts chained up,' he retorted in a forceful tone of voice. 'At the end of the day, our true nature revolves around two things – number one: survival; and number two: the satisfaction of our appetites, be they sexual or otherwise. When you strip everything away, our basic nature isn't that different from all the other animals. That's the reality, mate.'

After making his point, Roger took down more gulps of his pint of stout and then belched loudly. Even though he came from a well-off part of London he always tried to make out he was more raw and less posh than he actually was.

'I think you're wrong,' Sean replied. 'I think there's more meaning to our existence than mere survival and the satisfaction of our appetites.'

'I'm afraid I'm not wrong,' said Roger. 'The culture that we're brought up in dictates our social manners and behaviour. But when you strip all that away, man is a very base animal, no different from the rest. That's the reality – deal with it!'

Sean shook his head.

'We're actually very, very different from the animals,' he insisted.

'I'm afraid we're not,' said Roger.

'But I'm afraid we are,' said Sean. 'For one thing, we have reason. Animals don't have reason; they just live by instinct. We not only have reason, we also have an innate sense of what's morally right or wrong – an inbuilt sense of morality. Animals don't have that. Sorry to get religious but I also believe we were created in the image and likeness of God, and we're also spiritual beings. Animals are not. So we're above the animals.'

'That is total horse manure!' Roger snapped back. 'You need to study Charles Darwin. We are animals, descended from apes.'

'There's no hard evidence for that,' Sean replied.

Roger licked his lips in readiness to educate Sean on the facts of evolution.

'But there *is* hard evidence for it,' he insisted. 'I'm willing to explain to you how evolution works, and how ape became man, if you'd like to hear it.'

'I'm all ears,' said Sean.

Roger was delighted for the opportunity to unleash his knowledge of evolution on Sean. Before the trip he'd done some research on evolution in his university library – on the off-chance of getting into a discussion on the subject with Sean. For Roger, Darwinian theory was that great scientific discovery which completely debunked Christianity and the Bible's explanation of how man and the universe came to be – it was the ultimate weapon against Christianity.

'Evolution all boils down to the principles of natural selection and genetic mutation,' Roger began to explain. 'We can look at the rabbit as an example. Let's say 1,000 rabbits get attacked by predators until only two survive. The two that survived made it because they had better eyesight, better ears, longer legs to run with than the others. Let's say that these two rabbits breed and produce young; the young they produce will receive half the DNA – or genetic code – of the mother rabbit and half the DNA of the father rabbit. So, they'll receive the gifts that helped their parents survive predatory attacks, thereby helping them to survive too. This is how a species evolves into something superior than before. But DNA doesn't get passed on perfectly. There are always slight modifications that take place, so the offspring are never perfect copies of their parents. This difference between offspring and parent is known as genetic or DNA mutation. So, it's the combination of genetic gifts being continually enhanced through natural selection, as well as genetic mutation, that causes a species to change and evolve over time. Do you follow me?'

'Aye,' said Sean, 'I know what you're saying.'

'So, let's apply this to how apes became men,' said Roger. 'Through the natural selection process certain apes increased their intelligence and awareness, became more dextrous with their hands and developed a greater ability to communicate with sounds, eventually being able to speak. Along with this, continuous genetic mutation took place. The end result of all this was that, after several million years, ape became man! The proof that we descend from apes comes from the fact that our DNA so closely resembles other primates. In fact, we share ninety-eight per cent of our DNA with chimpanzees. Did you know that?'

'Aye, I've heard about it,' said Sean.

'I haven't,' Paul interjected.

'Well, then,' said Roger to Sean. 'The fact that we share ninety-eight per cent of our DNA with chimpanzees suggests we have a hell of a lot in common with them, and it's a fair bet that we also share a common ancestry with them, as we do with all other primates.'

A self-satisfied Roger then reached for his stout. He felt he'd just hit Sean for six with his eloquent explanation of Darwinian theory. However, an unflustered Sean was ready to answer back.

'We may share ninety-eight per cent of our DNA with the chimpanzee, but we also share fifty per cent of our DNA with the banana,' he calmly answered. 'Did you know that? Fifty per cent of what makes up a human being is what also makes up a banana. So, do we share a common ancestry with the banana?'

Roger was briefly silent. He needed a little think.

'Why not?' he eventually replied. 'After all, we evolved from apes, and apes evolved from other mammals, and mammals evolved from reptiles, and reptiles evolved from amphibians, and amphibians evolved from fish, and fish evolved from pond scum, and pond scum evolved from something else. So, it's feasible that we share a common source of beginning with bananas and other vegetation.'

An unperturbed Sean was ready with another response.

'But of all the prehistoric fossils that have been dug up, they still haven't found the missing link between us and our alleged ape ancestors, and that's probably because there aren't any to be found.'

'But I think you'll find they have found some,' a defiant Roger replied.

'No they haven't,' Sean insisted. 'And as for Charles Darwin, most of his theories have been blown out by modern science. Darwinian theory only works within the confines of individual creature groups. For example, you can have very different-looking breeds of dog that have been developed by selective breeding, but they still all remain dogs capable of breeding with one another because they all have compatible DNA structures, and the information is there in their genetic codes to make it happen. But two creatures with incompatible DNA structures obviously can't interbreed and there's no hard evidence that they can derive from the same ancestry. Apes cannot evolve into humans because the information isn't there in their DNA structures to make it happen. This idea that we're descended from apes depends on DNA structures, or genetic codes, being able to acquire radically new information from somewhere. But there's no hard evidence that either environmental factors or continuous genetic mutations can bring on this new information in the genetic code… even after millions and millions of years.'

'I wouldn't be so sure of that,' replied an unconvinced Roger. 'Most of the world's scientists would disagree with you.'

Then Paul had something to say.

'If Darwin's theories have been disproved, how come all these nature programmes we see on TV are always referring to him?' he asked. 'How come his name is always mentioned and they still seem so accepting of his ideas – that we're descended from apes, and so forth?'

'Maybe it's because his ideas *haven't* been disproved,' said Roger. 'Otherwise these programmes wouldn't advocate his ideas. I mean, why would they give out false information?'

'It isn't so much that they're giving out false information,' said Sean, 'the problem is they're giving you *selective* information. The information they give is from an extremely biased slant. The people who control our media are working to a hidden agenda. They don't want people to know the whole truth.'

'What do you mean, they have a hidden agenda?' Paul queried Sean.

'Our media, our universities, and in fact the world is more or less under the control of secular liberals,

Marxists, humanists and their various allies who have an agenda against Christianity and biblical teachings,' Sean asserted. 'A good umbrella term for these people would be "secularists". And the people who control the mass media despise Christianity. That's why nature programmes on TV promote evolution and completely unproven ideas about us being descended from apes, because it contradicts the biblical explanation of the origin of man.'

Roger lowered his eyebrows.

'That sounds like a paranoid conspiracy theory to me,' he answered.

'But I promise you there is little substance to the idea that we're descended from apes,' Sean reiterated. 'This idea that all living creatures derive from a common ancestry and just came about by a succession of random accidents is the most preposterous explanation for the origin of life. Yet this idea is being force-fed to us as though it were a proven fact. They just can't think of any better non-biblical explanation of man's origin other than Darwin's theory, which is seriously flawed.'

'Okay, then,' said Roger, 'what's the biblical explanation of man's origin?'

Sean briefly paused.

'The biblical explanation is that the first humans were created by an all-powerful, omnipotent Creator,' he replied. 'They did not evolve from apes or any other creatures. The first humans were Adam and Eve.'

'Adam and Eve?' Roger scoffed. 'You mean you actually believe the fairy tale about that man and woman in the Garden of Eden who wore nothing but fig leaves? Oh, and they were tempted into eating some forbidden fruit by a talking snake and that caused the fall of mankind or something!'

Sean nodded.

'Are you seriously telling me you actually believe Adam and Eve were real and their story is a true one?' Roger asked.

'Aye,' said Sean. 'I realise people have problems with Adam and Eve, but that's because they haven't had the story explained to them in a way that makes rational sense.'

'Do me a favour, then, and explain the story of Adam and Eve in a way that makes rational sense,' requested Roger.

'I'll try to,' said Sean before nervously taking a sip of his mineral water. This was a tricky subject matter to discuss. He knew his words had to be right.

'In the beginning,' he began, 'God – who is unlimited in power – created heaven, the universe, the earth and everything in it, out of absolutely nothing. And this, by the way, is the most rational explanation for how the universe, the earth and the first humans got here. At the end of the day, you've only really got two options – either an all-powerful Creator made it all, or *nothing* made it all! Take your pick!'

Roger turned to Paul and superciliously smirked before turning back to Sean. Whilst Sean was a bit irritated by this, he gathered himself and forged on with his explanation of the Adam and Eve story.

'In heaven, God created spirit beings called angels, giving them a high intelligence and free will. On earth, He created the animals and the first humans, Adam and Eve. Human beings were set apart from all other creatures because they were made in the image and likeness of God, and they were also given the gift of free will – which meant they could choose for good or for evil. As you mentioned, Adam and Eve lived in the Garden of Eden – which was a paradise. But God planted in this garden a tree of forbidden fruit and told Adam and Eve that they could eat of any tree in the garden except this one. God did this to test Adam and Eve's love and faithfulness to Him. But Adam and Eve decided to abuse the gift of free will by refusing to obey God and – persuaded by the devil, a fallen angel – they ate of the tree. Through their disobedience, humanity became separated from God and became cursed, and ever since then our world and the human race has suffered the consequences. Their sin brought about the fall of man. That's pretty much the story of Adam and Eve in a nutshell.'

An unimpressed Roger briefly stared at Sean before replying.

'No offence, but I think you're nuts, mate,' he said, bluntly. 'You actually think that the story of Adam and

Eve, which is as far-fetched as any fairy tale, gives a more rational explanation of the origin of man than Charles Darwin's theory?'

'I would say it's more rational when you study it closely,' said Sean. 'What is it specifically about the story that gives you problems?'

'I don't have any problems with it,' said Roger. 'I just don't think it's true. I don't think any sane, intelligent person would think it's true.'

'I'm with Roger,' said Paul. 'I think the story of Adam and Eve is a symbolic, allegorical story. I don't think it's meant to be taken literally.'

'You're wrong,' said Sean. 'There are parts of the Bible which are symbolic and not meant to be taken literally, but that isn't the case with Adam and Eve. The story of Adam and Eve is an historical reality. They were real people. They were as real as we are. They were the first humans – our first parents. People have a problem with Adam and Eve because they have a problem with the idea that the first humans, and indeed our universe, could be supernaturally created by an all-powerful Creator. But the most reliable scientific research, especially fossil evidence, appears to show that human beings appeared on this earth literally overnight and didn't evolve from other creatures... but they won't tell you this on TV nature programmes. Literally hundreds of thousands of fossils have been dug up and not only are there no reliable missing links found for humans, there are none for any other creatures either. Every time they think they've found a missing link it gets lots of excited media attention, but the finding always turns out to be either a big mistake or a fabricated hoax.'

'Wait a second,' said Roger. 'Only the other week I was in the library looking at a book on evolution and there were loads of diagrams and illustrations of missing link creatures that have been discovered, including the missing link between us and the apes, so I'm afraid you're wrong.'

Sean again was quick to answer.

'Those "missing link" illustrations were based on nothing more than wild speculation and wishful thinking. I promise you, they haven't discovered a single concrete example of a missing link. As far as missing links between us and the apes are concerned, they've never ever discovered anything more than an ape or less than a man. And even Charles Darwin himself admitted that his whole theory of evolution rested upon the discovery of intermediary fossils – which they still haven't found 120 years after his death!'

'Are you sure about all this?' asked a sceptical Roger.

'Aye, absolutely sure,' Sean responded. 'Humans did not evolve from apes or other living organisms and we did not "evolve" by accident. The body and workings of a human being are too intricately well designed to have been developed by evolution or random chance. There are just too many outrageous coincidences that must come together for us to have been created by evolutionary processes or by random chance.'

5

Creation or Accident?

After their drink at Molly Malone's, the three of them made their way over to another British pub – The Bull's Eye. This pub wasn't as traditional as either The Saint George or Molly Malone's and had more the feel of a modern bar. Roger had delayed taking Paul for his first visit around the red-light district because he wanted to continue his debate with Sean. After a less than dominant start, he was determined to get the upper hand. He decided he'd use a more direct, no-nonsense approach to attack Sean's beliefs and go for the jugular a bit more.

'Y'know, the chief reason why people believe in some divine Creator is because they *want* to believe in it,' Roger put forward. 'It all boils down to wishful thinking. But the reality is that there's no way of concretely proving the existence of God, so it's foolish to follow any religious system – whichever one it may be.'

'Are you an atheist, then?' Sean asked.

'I'm not really an atheist,' answered Roger. 'I'm an agnostic. That's the most logical, intelligent position to take, because the existence of God can neither be proved nor disproved.'

'I agree,' Paul concurred.

'But I would argue that we have emphatic evidence for the existence of a divine Creator,' Sean responded.

'D'you reckon?' said Roger.

'Aye,' said Sean. 'I could give you one piece of evidence after another to prove the existence of a Creator.'

'Let's hear them, then,' said Roger. 'I could do with a laugh.'

Sean sipped his fruit juice. Most of the nerves he'd had earlier on had now ebbed away and he was in a strong, confident mood to engage in argument.

'Let me give you one piece of scientific evidence off the top of my head,' he said.

'I'm all ears,' said Roger.

'Right,' Sean began, 'consider this: reliable scientific evidence tells us that if our world, Planet Earth, was tilted just one single mile closer to the sun we'd all be scorched to death. If the earth was just one single mile further away, we'd all freeze to death. How was it that the earth was positioned in exactly the right place in order for life to be sustained? Could the earth really have ended up in exactly the right position just by random chance?'

Roger had a brief think.

'Why not?' he eventually replied.

'Okay,' said Sean, 'let me give you something else. The chances of protein coming into existence by evolution or random chance alone have been calculated at ten to the 164th power to one.'

Sean then took a coin out of his pocket to make a point.

'Y'know, there are more chances of me flipping this coin and it landing on heads a hundred times in a row than for protein to have developed by pure chance,' he stated.

Roger remained unmoved.

'But it's actually *possible* for the coin to land on heads a hundred times in a row,' he responded. 'Granted, it's highly unlikely, but who's to say over millions or billions of years of trying it couldn't be done?'

'Okay,' said Sean, 'let me give you a couple of other things to think about. Let's look at the complexity of the cell. During Darwin's time, microscopes were a lot more primitive than they are today, so when Darwin looked at cells under a microscope he wouldn't have seen very much. But today's microscopes are a hundred times more powerful. We're now able to see all the intricate details of what makes up a cell – and what we find is incredible complexity that can only be the work of intelligent design, not chance. We can also look at DNA, specifically the DNA molecule. A single DNA molecule – which obviously can't be seen by the naked eye – is more complexly designed and possesses more information than the world's biggest and most sophisticated computer. This could not have come about by chance or evolution – it's impossible!'

An on-fire Sean briefly paused for thought before saying more.

'Let me give you more scientific evidence. There are seventeen "constants" that govern the universe. A constant is a fixed number that governs various physical functions within the universe. We have constants for space and time; we have energy constants, gravitational constants, cosmological constants, speed and light constants, etc. If any single one of these constants differed by the tiniest fraction the universe could not have developed the way it did and no life could have been sustained. I could go on and on all day giving you other proofs. At the end of the day, our creation couldn't have come about by random chance; the probabilities are just too out of this world and gargantuan for that to be the case.'

Roger still remained unbending.

'But who's to say it wasn't all created by the process of evolution, regardless of the staggering improbabilities?' he replied. 'I mean, we're talking billions and billions of years for it to happen. Time negates the improbability of it happening by chance.'

'But even if it was all created by evolution or natural selection, who or what gave us the process of evolution in the first place?' Sean asked. 'Evolution doesn't explain evolution. Even when you reduce everything to atoms and molecules you're still left with the question of where did they come from and who put the laws of physics in place to manipulate all these natural elements in the first place? There has to have been a primary source, a source of beginning, and that source of beginning can only be an omnipotent, intelligent designer – otherwise known as God.'

'But nothing you're saying is actually proving the existence of God,' Roger defiantly replied.

Sean scratched his head in frustration before making further points.

'Y'know, atheist materialists insist that all that existed in the beginning was dead matter. But how did that matter get here? Bearing in mind that something can't be produced by nothing, how did matter get here? Even Albert Einstein came to the conclusion that there had to be a Creator or intelligent designer working outside of the creation who put everything in place, and this Creator couldn't have been bound by the physical laws of nature that we're bound by. In other words, this Creator had to have been unlimited in power and with the ability to create out of nothing.'

'Okay, then,' said Roger, 'like I've already said, I'm an agnostic. I'm very open to the existence of God. But where's the proof for Christianity? Where's the proof for Jesus? Why are Christians so sure that Jesus is God and their religion is the correct one?'

Sean briefly puffed out his cheeks before answering.

'I can give you lots and lots of rational, logical evidence for Jesus Christ, but that mightn't mean much to you because first and foremost our faith in Christ depends on grace. That is, Jesus reaches out to us and we have to humbly respond to Him. Our faith revolves around a relationship of love and communion with Christ – it's an encounter. A person in a relationship with Jesus Christ has His Spirit – known as the Holy Spirit – dwelling within him and so knows He is God and knows He is Truth.'

'All this doesn't wash with me,' said Roger. 'I'm afraid you believing Jesus is God and Truth just because you feel His Spirit dwelling within you isn't enough to convince me. A Buddhist can say the same thing about Buddha. A Muslim can say the same about Allah. I need more tangible evidence than what you're giving me.'

'Okay,' said Sean, 'I'll give you one piece of supernatural evidence – my miraculous healing after my car accident. My family unceasingly prayed and begged Jesus for my life – and their prayers were answered. I was healed. Though, as you can see, I still have the physical scars to remind me of the experience.'

A sceptical Roger shook his head.

'With respect, do you have absolute proof that your healing was anything miraculous?' he retorted.

'Well, doctors and medical experts couldn't explain my recovery,' Sean insisted. 'They couldn't give an explanation at the time and they still can't explain it now. Even they admitted my recovery defied physiological laws. I can also tell you of other people experiencing astounding healings through the power of Christ.'

Roger shook his head again.

'Isn't it a medical fact that if you think you're going to get well you're much more likely to get well?' he proposed. 'If you're convinced Jesus or Buddha or some other god is going to heal you, that will naturally increase your chances of getting well. But the reality is that the person gets healed by the power of his own mind, not by any god or gods. They call it the placebo effect. Y'know, the mind can do incredible things.'

'I hear what you're saying,' said Sean, 'but in my case I was in a deep coma and practically dead to the world. I was reliant on the prayers of my family, not my own prayers, and not by the "power of my own mind" as you suggest.'

'But there has to be a rational, logical explanation for why you recovered,' Roger insisted.

'Well, the medical people couldn't find one,' Sean reiterated. 'Why not accept the possibility that I was miraculously cured?'

'Because I'm afraid I can't take your religion seriously,' said Roger. 'I can't take seriously the idea that the universe was created out of thin air or that the Adam and Eve story is real. It's just too crazy to accept.'

Sean had a brief think before coming back.

'When God created the universe and the world, he put in place natural, physical laws and a natural order, and they were put in place for our benefit. If you think about it, life would be pretty chaotic and difficult if we didn't have natural, physical laws, because they provide order and stability. But, as I said, God Himself is not bound by natural, physical laws – He is the Creator of them and is outside of them. In other words, He possesses supernatural power – and only God alone possesses supernatural power. And we're reminded of the supernatural power of God when miracles take place. A miracle is essentially an event or occurrence that defies natural, physical laws. So the universe, the world and the first humans were created in a miraculous, supernatural way simply because our God had the power to do so.'

'But you've got to be a bit simple to believe the Adam and Eve story is an historical fact,' Roger insisted. 'The story doesn't make any sense anyway. How does them eating some forbidden fruit bring about the fall of mankind? And you can't really blame them for having a bite – it was that wretched snake that talked them into it,' he added with sarcasm.

6

The Fall of Man

They decided to have another drink in The Bull's Eye before moving on. Paul got a round of drinks in, while Roger and Sean remained locked in debate over the subject of Adam and Eve. Roger saw Adam and Eve as a weak point that he could attack because to him it was so clearly nothing more than a fairy tale.

'Y'know, the Brothers Grimm would have been proud to have written the story of Adam and Eve,' Roger asserted. 'The whole thing is so clearly a mythological story and yet you think it was an actual historical event.'

Sean nodded.

'Aye, I do,' he said. 'I know that on the surface it might seem like a myth but, as I mentioned, Albert

Einstein came to the conclusion that there had to exist an omnipotent, all-powerful Creator who put everything together – and a great many other renowned scientists share that opinion. So, if you consider the idea that there exists a divine Creator for whom nothing is impossible, and who is unlimited in power and possesses supernatural power, then the supernatural and the miraculous become feasible – and the story of Adam and Eve becomes feasible.'

'And you actually think that the fall of the human race was caused by Adam and Eve eating some forbidden fruit in the Garden of Eden, and the talking snake that tempted them really existed?' Roger asked.

'The fall of the human race was caused by Adam and Eve's disobedience,' said Sean. 'By disobeying God, Adam and Eve made the decision to live independently from God. But God is the source of all goodness, so by wishing to live apart from Him they naturally brought evil upon themselves, becoming spiritually deformed and passing on this curse to their offspring – the human race. And that "talking snake" who tempted them was the devil.'

Roger grinned again.

'I'm afraid the devil is another piece of pure fiction,' he said. 'Just like Adam and Eve.'

'There's nothing fictional about the devil,' Sean sternly replied.

'The devil is nothing more than a man-made idea,' Roger insisted. 'The Church developed the idea of the devil and the idea of hell in order to psychologically manipulate people. They wanted to frighten people, to make them feel insecure and get them through their doors on a Sunday.'

Sean shook his head.

'You're wrong,' he countered. 'The devil is real. Believe me.'

'Have you seen him, then?' Roger asked, sarcastically.

'I've never seen him, because he's a spiritual being, without physical form,' said Sean. 'However, I've witnessed exorcisms where demonic spirits have been driven out of a person. I assure you, if you saw some of the things I've seen you'd have no problems in believing in the existence of the devil.'

'These "exorcisms" you saw were carefully staged hoaxes,' Roger answered. 'You were fooled, mate. Trust me on that. The Church stages these things to give their religion some sort of credibility. I guarantee you, what you saw wasn't genuine.'

'What I saw *was* genuine,' Sean responded. 'I also know people who have dabbled in witchcraft and the occult and lived to regret it. They played about with tarot cards and Ouija boards and very sinister things happened to them. You can't play around with things of the devil and not be affected. The devil is real and his menace to us is real.'

'You believe that nonsense cos you want to believe it,' Roger retorted, 'but there's no such thing as the devil. Get over it.'

'But if God is capable of creating human beings and all the animals of the earth, He's also capable of creating creatures not of this earth,' Sean pointed out, 'including the creature we know as the devil, or Satan.'

Roger rolled his eyes before Sean continued.

'The devil – or Satan – was originally a glorious angelic being, endowed with great gifts, and at first there was no evil in him because God is good and everything He creates is good. But this angel became self-absorbed and swollen with pride, and he ended up refusing to worship and serve God. Angelic beings, like human beings, were given the gift of free will, which meant that they, like humans, had the choice to put their trust in the all-loving God or rebel against Him. A third of the angels, led by the devil, made the choice to rebel because they wanted to be their own masters and be independent from God. Eventually, they were cast out of heaven and thrown into a domain that God specially created for them – the place known as hell – though they were also given the freedom to enter into our realm and ensnare as many human souls as possible to take with them to hell. Y'see, the devil wants to take us all down to hell out of spiteful hatred for God. Because he can't do any harm to God he sets his sights on us, as we're made in the image and likeness of God and infinitely loved by Him.'

'Sorry, but this all sounds like something out of a fantasy novel,' interjected Roger, who was not in the least bit impressed.

Sean ignored the remark and continued.

'As I said, the devil's not on his own. A third of the angels were cast out of heaven with him. They became his agents – commonly known as demons or evil spirits. These demons are in league with him, in his rebellion against God. The Bible and Church tradition teach us that the devil has the power to affect our imagination and tempt us, but he can't force us to do anything against our will; by God's grace we have the free will to either comply with or reject the devil's temptations. Having said that, no human being can stand up to him or outwit him on their own. None of us have a chance against him on our own. We can only keep him at bay by God's protective grace and by our co-operation with that grace.'

'You mentioned Church tradition. By that you mean the tradition of the Catholic Church, right?' queried Roger.

'Aye, that's right,' Sean replied.

'Well, what about the Anglican Church or the Methodist Church or the Mormon Church, etc?' Roger asked. 'What do the traditions of these churches say about devils and demons?'

'These other religious groups may have some different ideas, but they should be ignored because Jesus only established one Church and that was the Catholic Church,' Sean insisted.

'How d'you work that out?' asked Roger.

'There are lots of reasons why the Catholic Church is the one true Church, but I'll give you just two very good ones,' Sean proposed.

'Tell us,' said Roger.

'First of all, the Catholic Church is the only institution that can trace itself back 2,000 years,' Sean began. 'We know the names of every Pope going back to the first one – the apostle, Peter. However, no Protestant sect can trace itself back before the 1500s, and the Mormons and Jehovah's Witnesses can't trace themselves back before the 1800s. Secondly, in its 2,000-year history, the Catholic Church has never committed formal heresy. In other words, it's never officially changed its stance on any of its faith and moral teachings. This is not to say there hasn't been plenty of corruption, disobedience and rebellion within the Church throughout its history. But nonetheless, in spite of all the corruption, the Church has never backtracked on its dogmas or official teachings on faith and morals. However, all the major Protestant sects have altered their theological and moral teachings. For example, they now permit contraception and they permit divorce and remarriage – which are grave sins before God. So, for these reasons and others, I can strongly argue that the Catholic Church is the one and only Church established by Christ.'

'Yeah, right,' said Roger, not entirely convinced.

'These teachings I'm giving you about the devil and his demons come directly from the Church that Jesus Himself established, as well as the Bible,' Sean insisted. 'So the information I'm giving you is reliable and trustworthy.'

'If you say so,' said Roger, flippantly.

Sean then looked straight at Roger before firing some more words of warning.

'Getting back to the devil and his demons, I need to point out that whilst full-on demonic possession is pretty rare, demonic influence on the mind is commonplace – especially among those who wilfully reject Christ and His Church, because they're not spiritually protected. The devil can penetrate a person's subconscious without them knowing it. Your thought processes can be under the influence of the devil without you even realising it. And often he'll influence your thoughts in a very subtle way.'

'How naughty of him,' said a smiling Roger, still showing mocking contempt for what Sean was saying.

Sean, though, still had more to say.

'There are lots of ways in which a person can bring demonic influence into their lives. Playing about with Ouija boards, tarot cards, astrology, palmistry, Wicca, witchcraft, etc., all provide a gateway for the devil to get in. But any non-Christian activity or practice that puts you in an altered state of consciousness can make you vulnerable, such as hypnotism, Eastern meditation, yoga, Tai chi, and so on. These things are spiritually dangerous because they take you out of your normal state of consciousness and provide a space for the devil to get in. And I have to warn you that getting drunk or taking recreational drugs – like smoking weed – can also make you vulnerable for the same reasons.'

'Ha, ha, ha!' Roger guffawed. 'You've got more chance of knitting fog than of getting me to stop getting drunk or smoking weed. These are the main reasons we came to Amsterdam.'

'I'm with Roger on that,' said Paul with a smile.

Sean, though, remained insistent.

'The devil and his demons prowl this earth looking to invade souls,' he reiterated. 'If you give them an opening, they will enter.'

Then Paul had a question for Sean.

'If God is all-powerful and all-loving, why does He allow Satan to roam the earth and make all this trouble for us? To me, that doesn't make sense.'

'God gives the devil the freedom to roam our earth so he can tempt us and test us,' Sean replied, 'and by resisting his temptations we grow stronger spiritually and our love and trust for God can grow deeper. So the devil's presence here on earth is actually for our benefit, just as pain and suffering was brought into this world for our benefit, crazy as that sounds. Y'see, pain and suffering is a double-edged sword. It can purify us and bring us closer to God, or it can make us bitter and drive us further away from God. It all depends on how we react to it.'

Roger shook his head.

'I can't see anything beneficial about pain and suffering,' he said. 'It's a cruel God that allows all this suffering and misery in our world.'

'Suffering, misery and death came into the world

because of sin,' Sean explained, 'going all the way back to Adam and Eve when they ate the so-called "forbidden fruit". Though they may have been prompted by the devil, it was their decision, their choice, to eat of the tree. The instigating sin behind their decision to disobey God was the sin of pride. The devil told them that if they ate of the tree they would possess new knowledge and become like God, and they wanted this. They wanted to be their own masters, their own gods. So, in the same way that the sin of pride caused the fall of the devil, it also caused the fall of the first humans. This is why the sin of pride is often called the "mother of all sins". And the very essence of Satanism is pride and self-centredness – living by the principle that I am my own god and I can do exactly as I please! And really, what took place in the Garden of Eden served as a blueprint for all of human history. It represents in microcosm the whole story of humanity, because the history of the world has revolved around man insisting on doing things *his own way*, in defiance of the Creator, and therefore continuously enduring the consequences of his pride and his rebellion against God.'

Sean then briefly paused for thought before saying more about pride.

'Nothing separates us from God more than the sin of pride. Pride is basically self-worship – when we think we know what's best and know more than our Creator. But when we reject God, He rejects us. When we make the free-will choice to disown God, He respects that decision and in turn will disown us, leaving us to go to our own self-inflicted doom. From start to finish, the Bible tells us that God always distances Himself from the proud, but to the humble He always stays close; He will always watch over and bless the humble.'

'And who exactly are the "humble"?' asked Roger.

'The humble are people who know their limitations and recognise that there is something much bigger and much higher than themselves,' answered Sean. 'It's as simple as that.'

7

The Price of Free Will

After leaving The Bull's Eye, Roger again delayed taking Paul on his first tour of the red-light district as he felt a little peckish, so he took Paul and Sean to a pancake restaurant by the name of *Pannenkoekenhuis de Van Zyl* (Van Zyl's Pancake House), situated on the Damrak. On Roger's advice, the three of them ordered Dutch apple pancakes and they all happily munched. In the midst of their eating, both Roger and Sean were quiet, wanting a breather from their debating. However, Paul wanted their discussion to resume. He found their exchanges quite interesting and entertaining. After chewing down his final mouthful of pancake, he had something to say about Adam and Eve – with the hope of getting the debate going again.

'Y'know, I still don't get why the whole human race was cursed with suffering and death just because Adam and Eve munched on a bit of fruit they were told not to. It seems a bit harsh.'

Roger rolled his eyes, knowing that Paul's comment was about to kick things off again. Meanwhile, Sean chewed down his last bit of pancake before answering Paul's remark.

'The great sin of Adam and Eve was that they had decided to no longer put their trust in God. What they did through their disobedience was tell God that they no longer needed Him in their lives.'

Sean then briefly paused for thought before saying more.

'Rejection of God had its consequences for Adam and Eve, and their offspring – the human race. Death, disharmony and suffering were brought into the world because humanity became separated from God. The separation brought physical, emotional and spiritual curses on humanity – known collectively as the curse of original sin.'

'The curse of original sin?' said Paul. 'I remember learning about that. It's the curse we apparently all inherit from Adam and Eve, right?'

'Aye,' said Sean. 'The curse of original sin means we're all born with rebellious, corrupted, selfish natures, inclining us to sin. And this sinful nature we are born with is our most frightening enemy – it's a bigger enemy to us than the devil and his demons because it's due to our weakened, sinful nature that we so often cave in to the devil's temptations.'

'But what exactly is "sin"?' asked Roger. 'I mean, one man's sin is another man's pleasure. And who has the right to define what sin is? I actually don't even think there's any such thing as sin.'

'Sin is simply the breaking of God's laws,' answered Sean.

'Yeah, you mean the breaking of God's laws according to the Catholic Church,' Roger responded. 'And this business that we're all born with the curse of original sin is yet another utterly bizarre piece of Church-invented fiction.'

'The curse of original sin is a reality,' Sean insisted.

'If you say so,' said Roger.

Sean ignored Roger's contempt for what he was saying and proceeded to say more on the subject of original sin as he sensed Paul taking him a little more seriously.

'Original sin is a genetic curse, handed down from generation to generation,' he explained. 'It took thousands and thousands of years before God finally sent us Someone to set us free from this curse – that Person was His Son, Jesus Christ, who by His sacrifice on the cross paved the way for all of mankind to be saved. What Christ did by His sacrifice was purchase the grace for all of us to be delivered from our sins and escape the eternal damnation we justly deserve. It's down to us to make the free-will choice to co-operate with the grace merited for us by Christ – which God gives all of us – in order to overcome our sins, attain holiness and inherit heaven. It must be understood that original sin twisted us out of shape. Christ came down to earth to twist us back into shape, to restore us back to God.'

'Yeah, whatever,' said Roger, again diverting his eyes to Paul and smirking.

Sean felt the need to say more about God's grace.

'Like I've said, God gives everyone the grace to be saved, but most people reject His grace. This is the terrible price of free will – that people have the option to reject His grace and therefore be damned. And I would say that most people say no to Jesus because they don't fancy the demands that being a Christian would place on them. Being a Christian means actively seeking to put away all sin from your life and striving for holiness in co-operation with God's grace. It means moving from pride to humility; it means moving from selfishness to selflessness; it means moving from being unforgiving to being forgiving and compassionate; it means moving from vice to virtue; it means moving from impurity to purity; it means living according to the spirit as opposed to the flesh; ultimately, it means making a conscientious effort to overcome the effects of original sin. But because original sin twisted us out of shape, it's a painful process for us to be twisted back into shape – it involves suffering and dying to yourself – and most people aren't prepared to suffer and die to themselves.'

'But this is what really gets me,' said Roger. 'What's the point of life if it revolves around suffering and "dying" to yourself? Why does God, who you describe as all-loving, want us all to lead such miserable lives? I don't get it.'

'You've misunderstood me,' Sean replied. 'God doesn't want anyone to lead a miserable life. He wants us all to lead good, holy lives. But leading a good, holy life sometimes means being prepared to suffer and go through discomfort in order to do what's good and what's right. And I've never met a solid, faithful, practising Catholic who I would describe as "miserable". In fact, they're quite the opposite. They're the most joyful, inwardly most happy people you could meet. Y'see, living by Christ's teachings, as taught by His Church, always leads to internal joy and peace – a peace that money can't buy – regardless of any hardship or discomfort the person might be going through.'

Roger, however, wasn't buying Sean's proposition.

'This is another little trick that the Church tries to pull,' he countered, 'to tell people that being prepared to suffer is good for the soul, etc. It's nothing less than manipulation. If you convince people that suffering and hardship are good for the soul then it becomes very easy to manipulate them and make use of them.'

Sean remained silent, finding it very difficult to get through to someone as cynical and distrusting as Roger. Then Paul had a question.

'You describe God as all-loving? Why then does He send anyone who refuses to obey Him to hell? Isn't that a bit vengeful and spiteful?'

'God doesn't send anyone to hell,' said Sean. 'People put themselves there by choosing to live their lives outside of His grace and goodness. Like I said, all goodness comes from God. Hell is hell because it's totally devoid of God's goodness – that's what makes it such a dreadful, terrible place.'

'But if your God is all-powerful and all-loving, can He not ensure that no one ever goes to hell?' asked Roger.

'Let me again make it clear that God didn't create anyone for hell,' said Sean. 'He created us to be with Him in heaven forever, to be in a relationship of love and communion with Him forever. But He gave us minds and wills of our own to decide whether or not to be in this relationship for the simple reason that *love cannot be forced*. We're not robots that God can programme to love Him or be obedient to Him. God will not mind control us to love Him and choose Him, because we're not machines, we're free-will beings.'

Paul pondered on what Sean had said before asking him another question.

'Is it possible for someone who ends up in hell to get out of it?'

Sean solemnly shook his head before he answered.

'There is no chance of anyone in hell getting out. Church dogma and the Bible are quite clear on this.

Once you're down there, there's no getting out. Hell is a domain that's completely cut off and separated from God. Therefore the graces of God aren't there to make it possible for anyone to get out.'

'So, people who end up there remain there for all eternity?' asked Roger.

'Aye, I'm afraid so,' Sean answered. 'But you must remember that they end up there by their own free-will choice. They made the decision during their earthly life to reject God and rebel against the grace that came to them. Therefore, their damnation is just and deserved.'

'That does it,' said Roger. 'There's no way your religion can be true. How can God be all-loving and yet allow someone to rot away in hell for all eternity? No one – I don't care who they are or what they've done – deserves to suffer in hell forever. If God allows people to rot in hell forever, He either cannot be all-loving or He cannot be all-powerful.'

'I'm with Roger,' Paul agreed. 'It seems too harsh for someone to be punished for all eternity. No one deserves that, no matter what they've done.'

Sean remained silent. He couldn't think of much more to say on the issue.

'Sorry, Sean, but in my opinion all this stuff you're coming out with is just pure man-made, made-up hogwash,' said Roger, irreverently. 'I don't wanna be disrespectful, but I really think you've been duped into believing all this nonsense. You've been brainwashed.'

There wasn't any more Sean could say. It seemed his attempts at evangelising weren't quite having the desired effect on Roger and Paul he'd hoped for. For the rest of their stay in the restaurant he was subdued, not saying much.

Eventually, the three of them left the pancake restaurant. Roger and Paul parted from Sean to make their way over to the red-light district. They agreed to meet up later for supper at another restaurant.

8

Dope-Smoking Serpents

After leaving the pancake restaurant, Roger and Paul had headed right into the heart of the red-light zone. It seemed Sean's words of warning about the devil, sin and hell hadn't put them off.

The two of them were now sitting inside Steenkamp's Coffee House – a typical Amsterdam coffee shop which sold cannabis – and smoking ready-made Thai grass joints (a joint being a mix of cannabis and tobacco). Since the Dutch government had relaxed its laws on "soft" drugs in the 1970s, in order to regulate and control its use, the Dutch coffee shop had become one of the great pulls attracting foreign tourists to the country. It had certainly always been one of the great attractions enticing Roger to Amsterdam, and Steenkamp's had become a favourite haunt of his. Inside, a tall, Surinamese man with long dreadlocks was serving at the counter, and heavy reggae music was thumping in the background.

The visit to the coffee shop had come after Roger had shown Paul around De Wallen – the red-light district – for the very first time. He'd shown him around all the main streets and canals of the area, which included a walk around the infamous Oudezijds Voorburgwal canal. Roger had pointed out to Paul all of his favourite X-rated clubs and led him inside his favourite X-rated shops (where they indulged in as much magazine browsing as they could get away with). Paul had been stunned at how graphic and explicit the pornographic images in the shop windows were – and in broad daylight! And now he was indulging in another of Amsterdam's popular vices.

'Ahhh, this is the life, eh?' said Roger, after taking a long drag of his joint. 'Isn't this place fantastic? There's absolutely everything here that a man could want. All the pleasures you could ask for in just one little patch of a city.'

'Yeahhh,' said Paul, his eyes already glazed after just a few puffs.

'I was just thinking,' said Roger, 'our holier-than-thou, Bible-thumper friend doesn't know what he's missing.'

Paul smiled and nodded.

'Yeah,' he agreed, 'he's missing out on all this. But like I said earlier, each to his own. If he doesn't want to indulge in all this, that's his business.'

'Mind you,' said Roger, 'we need to be careful. Remember what he said about smoking this stuff. If we do it too much we can open the door to Satan. Ha, ha, ha.'

Paul laughed at Roger's sarcasm, but not too much. A small part of him was open to the possibility that Sean might be right.

Roger had another puff on his joint, then an idea came into his head.

'I reckon we should try to persuade Sean to give all this a go,' he proposed to Paul. 'I mean, it wouldn't do him any harm to let his hair down just once, eh? There's all these wonderful vices on offer and he keeps right away from them because of his religion. I reckon we should do all we can to release him from the shackles of that mundane, repressive religion of his.'

'You got to hand it to him, though,' said Paul, 'he certainly sticks by his principles and morals. I respect him for that.'

'You talk about him as though you like him,' said Roger.

'I do like him,' Paul admitted. 'Whatever you think about his religious convictions, he's a really nice guy. He's genuine.'

Roger was briefly silent.

'Don't you feel a bit sorry for him, though?' he said. 'I mean, he's missing out on all of the best things in life, all because of that stupid, square religion of his.'

'What makes you say his religion is stupid?' Paul asked. 'How do you know his beliefs aren't correct?'

'What?' Roger said sharply. 'Don't tell me you're turning into a Jesus freak as well?'

'No,' replied Paul, 'I just think you need to keep an open mind over spiritual matters. You have to be open to the possibility that his beliefs might be right and the explanation of creation he gave might be true.'

'What, you think that fantasy story about Adam and Eve is actual fact and not fiction?' questioned Roger.

'Well, he gave reasonable evidence to support the idea that we were created and didn't come to exist by accident,' Paul reminded Roger. 'So if we were created, who's to say the human race didn't start with Adam and Eve? The human race has to have started with someone.'

'I don't believe it,' said Roger. 'He's really turning your head, isn't he?'

'No, he's not turning my head,' Paul insisted. 'All I'm saying is that we need to keep an open mind about it.'

'Huh,' Roger grunted. 'No doubt we'll have another dose of him trying to brainwash us with his ideas at the restaurant tonight. As I said, I reckon we should do all we can to persuade him to give the red-light attractions a go. He needs to experience these pleasures for himself to realise what he's missing.'

Paul remained silent.

'Let's be like the snake in the Garden of Eden and tempt him into eating Amsterdam's forbidden fruits,' added Roger, mischievously. 'Let's tell him about the wonders of drinking beer and puffing on one of these.'

Roger had a drag on his Thai grass before continuing.

'Then we'll tell him about all the gorgeous babes in the brothels offering their services – all at reasonable prices! He'll surely be a little bit tempted. I mean, he's human. He must surely have a breaking point?'

'You can count me out of thh-at,' said Paul, beginning to slur his words due to the effects of his smoking. 'I'm not gonna tempt anyone into ss-inning.'

'You what?' Roger barked. 'You think that enjoying all these delights is sinning, do you?'

Paul had to think before replying.

'No, it's… it's not ss-inning. But it doesn't feel rr-ight to push someone like Shh-ean into the thh-ings that we're into. I thh-ink it would bring bad karma on us.'

'Bad karma?' said Roger, also now beginning to drag his words. 'I totally disagree. I rr-eckon we'd be doing him a favour if we persuaded him to jj-ust cut loose and enjoy himself ff-or a change. Besides, he's happy to preach to us his Christianity; why can't we preach to him our way of "anything goes" liberalism?'

Paul took a drag on his joint and thought about it.

'Maybe you're rr-ight,' he conceded. 'Perhaps it wouldn't do him any harm to indulge in life's amusements jj-ust once. But I doubt you'll persuade him. He seems to have cast-iron willpower.'

'Well, let's give it a go anyway,' said Roger with enthusiasm. 'Thh-ere's no harm in trying. Let's bombard him with thh-oughts and pictures of the pleasures and vices of Amsterdam. Let's rr-eally get to work on his mind. We'll make that ss-nake in the Garden of Eden look like an amateur. Who knows, with enough poking and prodding of his imagination, he might jj-ust crack!'

9

The "Bit by Bit" Principle

It was evening. Roger and Paul had staggered back to the hotel to fetch Sean for a bite to eat at Mae Wong's, a small Chinese restaurant situated in Amsterdam's Chinatown, just on the outskirts of the red-light district. This was a favourite eating place of Roger's.

In the restaurant all three of them ordered noodles and were hungrily awaiting their meals. It had been a couple of hours since Roger and Paul had smoked their last joints and the effects were gradually wearing off. They were set to further regain their faculties by consuming some greasy Chinese grub, with its capacity to lessen the effects of both alcohol and weed. Although the restaurant served beer, they wisely chose to switch to fruit juice while having their meals. Roger then began to get to work on trying to tempt Sean into joining him and Paul in the red-light area later.

'Isn't the red-light district absolutely fantastic?' he said to Paul, glancing at Sean to make sure he was listening.

'Yeah,' said Paul, 'it was certainly interesting.'

'And you've only seen it during the day, when not a lot happens,' said Roger. 'Wait till I show you around tonight. It really comes alive after dark. You'll see the ladies of the night for the first time.'

Roger again glanced at Sean, to see if his words were making any impression on him.

'Yeah, it's an experience everyone should go through at least once in their life,' he continued. 'I mean, you can't come to Amsterdam and not have at least one look around its world-famous red-light district. That would be like going to New York and not bothering to see the Statue of Liberty, or going to Paris and not seeing the Eiffel Tower. Aren't you even a little bit curious, Sean?'

'Not really,' Sean replied. 'I'm still keeping away.'

'But you're practically in the red-light area now,' said Roger. 'When you step outside of this restaurant you can see a couple of brothels just up this street. So why not let us take you on a quick tour? What harm would it do?'

'No, I'm not interested,' Sean said again, well aware he was being tempted. 'I honestly don't fancy walking around that modern-day Sodom.'

'What if we just take you around Oudezijds Voorburgwal?' Roger proposed. 'That's the main canal of the red-light district – the busiest bit. It won't take long to walk around.'

'No thanks!' Sean firmly repeated.

Despite Sean's adamant refusals, Roger wasn't about to give in that easily.

A waiter brought them their noodles and they all tucked in.

A little time passed, and while they were in the middle of their meals another devious idea came into Roger's head. *Perhaps one way*, he thought, *to get Sean more open and relaxed would be to get some alcohol in him.*

'So, have you never had a drink in your life, Sean?' Roger asked. 'When I say a drink, I'm talking about something alcoholic.'

'Aye, I've taken alcohol,' Sean admitted.

'Really?' said a surprised Roger. 'I thought drinking was against your religion.'

'Well, Catholics are allowed to enjoy alcohol in moderation,' Sean informed Roger. 'But during my teenage years I must admit I strayed completely from my faith and became a heavy drinker and even smoked a little.'

'My!' said Roger. 'You've never mentioned that before! All your secrets are coming out!'

'What made you give it up?' Paul asked.

'It was after my accident,' said Sean. 'I found my faith again and the need to drink just went away.'

'But as a Catholic you don't need to abstain from drink,' said Roger. 'And besides, didn't Jesus turn water into wine?'

Sean smiled, appreciating Roger having some knowledge of the Gospel.

'Abstaining from alcohol just feels good for me, though,' he replied. 'It's purely a personal decision.'

'But if Jesus had a little drink now and then, surely it wouldn't be a sin for you to have a small glass of beer?' said Roger, pushing it. 'And take it from me, Dutch beer is the tastiest in the world. You've got to try it while you're here! It's dead tasty, isn't it, Paul?'

'It is really nice,' Paul agreed.

'What d'you say, Sean?' said Roger. 'How about a glass of the old liquid gold?'

'No thanks,' Sean replied, decisively. 'I'm quite happy with my fruit juice.'

A frustrated Roger frowned at Sean's stubbornness.

'I dunno,' he said. 'I really can't understand you. No offence, but what's the point of your life and what's the point of living if you can't enjoy the pleasures of this world?'

'I do enjoy some of the pleasures of this world,' said Sean. 'I'm currently enjoying this tasty plate of chow mein.'

'I'm talking about *real* pleasures,' said Roger. 'I'm talking about booze, drugs and sexual amusement.

These are the best things that life has to offer – and you're saying no to them because of that oppressive, miserable, self-denying religion of yours.'

'A good life doesn't depend on earthly pleasures,' Sean retorted. 'A person can have an infinite amount of booze and drugs and sexual amusement at his disposal and yet still lead a very empty, unsatisfying life. And Christianity – that is, Catholicism – isn't an anti-pleasure religion. Catholicism recognises that all pleasures are a gift from God, including the enjoyment of alcohol and sex.'

'So, you're admitting these pleasures are a gift from God, yet you won't indulge in them yourself?' queried Roger.

Sean chewed down a mouthful of chow mein before replying.

'What I'm trying to say is that any given pleasure is not evil or sinful in and of itself. Pleasures only become sinful when we abuse them, causing harm to ourselves or others.'

Roger then decided to get blunt.

'No disrespect, but I think you're allowing your religion to stop you from living life to the full. It's really sad that you're letting ancient rules and commandments of your religion get in the way of enjoying life.'

'Obedience to my faith doesn't stop me from leading a good life,' Sean insisted. 'In fact, I'd say my faith helps me to appreciate the good things of this world more than most. And God's divine laws and commandments may be ancient but they're eternal. They stand forever. If you break God's commandments, they'll break you!'

Roger shook his head and smirked cynically.

'Sorry, but the laws and commandments you live by have absolutely no relevance in this day and age,' he argued. 'We've gone way beyond all that now.'

Sean in turn shook his head.

'God's divine laws and commandments still have relevance,' he replied. 'In fact, never more so than today. Our world is going to pot because we no longer take God's laws seriously. Look at Western society – how depraved and debauched it's become.'

'Why? Because it's become liberated and done away with Victorianism and repression?' Roger fired back. 'And because it's broken off the shackles of your oppressive religion?'

'Society has not liberated itself,' Sean asserted. 'By rejecting God's laws, society has created more traps and bondages for itself. Western society has gone backwards since its move away from traditional Christian values.'

'D'you reckon?' said Roger, disdainfully.

'Aye,' replied Sean. 'Since our society has "liberated" itself, we now have record numbers of people committing suicide, record numbers with addiction problems, record numbers suffering from depression, stress, mental illness and psychosomatic disorders. Society is more uncaring and aggressive. Sexual immorality is rife. We've seen the breakdown of the family with sky-rocketing divorce rates and single parent families now almost seen as normal. Worst of all is the diminishing respect for human life illustrated by the wiping out of millions of innocent lives through abortion. The biggest holocaust in human history is taking place right now in this era you're claiming to be so liberated!'

'I think you're exaggerating things just a little bit, Sean!' said Roger. 'I don't think our world is quite as bad as you're making out.'

'Really?' said Sean. 'Y'see, we can't appreciate how bad things have become because changes occur so gradually that we don't really notice the decay taking place. We accept today's moral decay because in a sense we don't know any better. We've been slowly conditioned to accept it. But little by little, bit by bit, our culture has deteriorated – and we barely realise it! The secularists in control of our world have used this "bit-by-bit" principle, changing the culture one step at a time with very clever methods of social engineering. They get us to tolerate a minor change before pushing the boundaries further and further until a radical change is brought about. It is by this method that abnormal things, such as abortion and pornography, can be pushed onto society and eventually get accepted as "normal".

'You keep going on about these "secularists" corrupting our world,' said Roger. 'Who exactly are these "secularists" you keep going on about? What exactly is their motive for wanting to corrupt us all?'

Sean had a little think before replying.

'Most secularists would describe themselves as people who reject the supernatural and live by science and reason alone, but I would describe them as people who reject God because they don't want to be bound by absolute truth and morals – that's the more accurate way to describe them. That's why they hate most religion, especially Christianity, and they hate dogmatic laws and boundaries. They think the key to happiness comes from being able to do whatever you want, and they think every individual is effectively his or her own god. The secularist movement first grew to prominence in the 18th century, and they've steadily increased their power since then through gaining control of the world of business and finance. When you control finance, it gives you power to control everything else, including the mass media. And you can plainly see that our mass media has a clear agenda against Christianity and biblical morals. And, let me repeat, the move away from biblical morals has happened slowly but steadily and very deliberately.'

'With respect, I think you're talking nonsense,' Roger said bluntly.

'But you only have to look at what's on our TV screens today,' said Sean. 'What would have been considered X-rated material forty years ago we can now see on our TV screens first thing in the morning. From the 1960s to the '70s to the '80s to the present, society has slowly been conditioned and forced to move away from our Christian values. You look at most of the soap operas, dramas and sitcoms we now see on TV – they all push the secularist agenda and promote anti-Christian morals. These programmes promote fornication, homosexuality, contraception, abortion, the feminist agenda, anti-patriarchy, etc. They promote all the things that attack both the family and the Church – the very two institutions that the devil is hell-bent on destroying. And I suspect the real driving force behind secularists' support of these things is more their hatred of Christianity than love of their fellow man.'

'Hang on,' said Roger. 'You're complaining about stuff on TV because it doesn't go well with your particular morals and religious beliefs. But no one has the right to dictate to us what are good morals and what are bad morals. Not everyone's moral guidelines are the same. An individual's morality differs from person to person. What's bad for some may be good for others, and vice versa.'

'I completely disagree,' Sean responded. 'Morals are absolute, not relative. Absolute morality exists because absolute truth exists, and the fullness of truth is found in God Himself.'

'Well, I'm afraid I don't agree with that,' said Roger. 'So it looks like we'll just have to agree to disagree.'

'The problem with a society that won't recognise the existence of God or a divine Lawgiver or a natural moral law is that moral boundaries become man-made, and the boundaries can change according to the whims of those in power,' Sean stated. 'Those in power can play God and dictate to us what is right or wrong because we have no base, no building block, no first principles to build upon. But deep down, every human being knows right from wrong, and good from bad, because we were all created in the image and likeness of God – who, as I said, is Truth itself. God created every human being with an innate sense of His natural law, and the human race retained this sense of right and wrong in spite of the curse of original sin and us being inflicted with a weakened, sinful nature. We all have a sense of right and wrong – commonly known as common sense – regardless of our religious or cultural backgrounds. We also all have an inbuilt sense of what is just and what is decent.'

'That is utter rubbish!' Roger snapped back. 'Our morals are forced on us from the day we're born. Things like culture, law, religion and upbringing determine the morals of an individual. We're not born with any sense of morality. There's no such thing as good or bad morals. Morals are just rules and guidelines that have, by and large, been drilled into us by the outside world. That's the reality – deal with it!'

'So, in your view, there's no such thing as absolute morality or absolute truth?' asked Sean.

'No,' said Roger bluntly.

'In that case, if you don't believe there are any absolute morals, there was nothing absolutely wrong with what Adolf Hitler did,' Sean proposed, 'or with what Ivan the Terrible did, or with what Jack the Ripper did. In fact, there can be nothing concretely wrong with any evil action, be it murder or theft or rape or anything else, right?'

'I'm not saying that,' said Roger, defensively.

'But you're saying that all morality is relative, so you can't condemn anyone for anything because you have no absolute standard of what is moral and what is right,' said Sean. 'Therefore, in intellectual honesty, you can't say to a rapist or a murderer that he's done anything wrong.'

Roger shook his head but remained silent. He was stuck for a response.

10

The New Paganism

The three of them moved on to Molly Malone's – the Irish pub they'd visited earlier. It wasn't long after settling down with their drinks that they got going again with the conversation they'd had at the restaurant – with Roger determined to get the upper hand!

'I completely disagree that our world has gone down the pan since moving away from Christianity,' he told Sean. 'We've actually moved in the right direction since moving away from religion and superstition. We've become more mature, more rational, more sane. And this move away from religion happened naturally. Evolution guided us this way. We advanced, grew more intelligent and naturally evolved towards no longer needing religion.'

Sean shook his head.

'I think you're wrong,' he answered. 'I don't think the move away from religion took place naturally or by any process of evolution.'

'So, why is the Western world so dismissive of God and religion now?' Paul asked. 'Or to put it another way, where did secularism come from?'

Sean paused for thought.

'It goes back to the Enlightenment,' he then answered, 'which was a philosophical movement that took place in Western Europe in the 18th century. Modern-day secularism can be traced back to this movement.'

'The Enlightenment?' queried Paul.

'Aye,' said Sean. 'The Enlightenment was a philosophical movement that elevated science, reason and naturalism above religion and the supernatural.'

'Quite right, too,' said Roger, before Sean continued.

'Enlightenment philosophers, such as John Locke, David Hume, Voltaire and others, pushed the idea that truth could only be known by what could be scientifically proven. They believed we had to rely on purely natural explanations for understanding life and the universe. All knowledge had to be science-based, and man had to live by human reason alone. Many of them dismissed the existence of mystery and the supernatural, insisting that nothing was beyond human understanding and that everything had the potential to be understood by the human mind. Along with this was also a denial of grace. They dismissed the idea that man and all other creatures are dependent on God's grace for everything, including their very existence. So whilst most of them believed in a Creator who set everything in motion, they believed this Creator to be impersonal, not having much to do with His creation. It was ideas such as these that led the world to a practical atheism.'

'Well, as far as I'm concerned, the Enlightenment was a movement that made a lot of sense and made the world a much saner place,' said Roger.

'But a major reason why this movement really took off in 18th-century Europe was because Christianity had become so weakened by the religious wars between Catholics and Protestants,' Sean pointed out. 'The Protestants themselves splintered into lots of different denominations, being unable to agree on their beliefs and doctrines. It was all this division and fragmentation that confused and weakened the Christian faith and paved the way for the secularist takeover.'

Sean paused again for thought, before continuing.

'Another major reason why the Enlightenment grew in strength was because the movement managed to exert great influence over the world of business and finance. I touched on this earlier. What we saw in the 18th century was the emergence of a new, liberal form of capitalism which was influenced by ideas that came out of the Enlightenment. This form of capitalism was based on free, unregulated trade and business practices – no longer restricted by monarchy or government – allowing individuals to amass as much wealth for themselves as they could, and this eventually concentrated wealth into the hands of the few – more specifically, the banks! In turn, those who gained control of this new, global capitalist system promoted and supported the liberal, anti-religious philosophies of the Enlightenment because many of its ideas accommodated their greed and lust for wealth. Y'see, true Christianity teaches that we must lead lives of sacrifice and self-denial for the good of others, and this is at odds with modern capitalism which is driven by consumerism and the pursuit of selfish gain. This really lies at the heart of why Christianity was increasingly pushed out; those who gained control of the world economy wanted it pushed out!'

'I don't buy what you're saying,' said Roger. 'The main reason we did away with Christianity was because in the aftermath of the Enlightenment we learnt to scrutinise and question everything. We learnt to use our intelligence in an honest, truthful way and see things for how they really are. In the same way that science and technology advanced, our understanding of how to look at the world advanced with it. We grew up, we matured and started to see the world with realistic, truthful eyes. The Enlightenment movement was maybe the greatest thing that ever came to humanity because it led us to realism and truth.'

Sean briefly closed his eyes and puffed out his cheeks.

'But it didn't lead us to truth,' he adamantly replied. 'Y'see, Enlightenment thinkers insisted that man needed to depend on science and reason alone and steer clear of religion and the supernatural, but it never dawned on them that by rejecting the supernatural they were actually being very unscientific and untruthful. If science is the bastion of truth it must be open to all possibilities, including the possible truth that there's such a thing as mystery, that there's such a thing as the supernatural. Science must also concede to the possible truth that there are things beyond human understanding. It also takes at least as much faith to think that science and human reason can explain everything as it does to follow any religious system.'

Roger shook his head with that familiar cynical smile on his face.

'But let's just look at things with realistic and truthful eyes,' he answered. 'At the end of the day, it's nothing more than insecurity and desperation that drives people to religion. Religion is nothing more than a crutch for helpless, desperate people. That's the reality!'

Sean sipped his mineral water before replying.

'The same argument works the other way. People who lead secure, comfortable lives can easily take their blessings for granted and turn from God. And Western society, which for centuries was shaped by Christian morals and civility, has now never had it so good. It is now, in this age of abundance and material well-being, that we should be honouring God more than ever. Instead, we've gone the other way; we're treating Him with contempt. We've become immersed in a neo-pagan culture, marked by idolatry and decadent morals.'

'Hang on a minute,' said Roger. 'Are you trying to tell me that there was no immorality in the world when it was dominated by Christianity? What about the Crusades, the Spanish Inquisition, witch-burning, black slavery, the medieval tyranny of the Catholic Church, the massacring of South American Indians who wouldn't convert to Christianity? I could go on and on.'

Sean was briefly silent. He took another sip of his mineral water.

'Aye,' he then said, 'I'll admit that throughout history Christians have succumbed to the sinful nature and the devil and have done bad things, and they haven't always lived by their teachings.'

'Yeah, just a bit,' interrupted Roger, before Sean continued.

'But what you have to remember is that whenever Christians have behaved badly, such as with witch-burning or with forcing Indians to accept Christianity or whatever, they were always going against the morals and teachings of their faith. In the case of the Crusades, Europe would have ended up completely overrun by Islam if they hadn't taken place – so from the Christian point of view they were absolutely necessary – though

I'll admit that some Crusaders did bad things. But the history of Christianity has always been the story of those who understood the basics of their faith and those who sadly didn't.'

'Whether Christians who did wrong knew they were doing wrong is irrelevant,' said Roger. 'Wrong is wrong regardless as to whether the person realises it or not.'

'Aye, but I'm actually trying to make a point,' said Sean. 'Y'see, whenever Christians committed evil they were always contradicting their faith. They were always acting outside the moral bounds of their faith. Now, compare that to the evil and atrocities committed by secular atheist governments such as the Nazis in Germany or the communists in Russia and elsewhere. Secularists or atheists believe there's no such thing as absolute morality; in other words, all morals are relative. So when Hitler murdered all those Jews, by his own moral code he didn't do anything wrong. Likewise, when Joseph Stalin got rid of millions of Russians who didn't agree with communism, by his own moral guidelines he did nothing wrong. When atheists commit evil they're not violating any moral code of their own because they believe all morality is relative and nothing is concretely evil. Therefore, there's no cut-off point to the evil they can perpetrate, and virtually any evil action can be justified.'

'Was there much of a cut-off point to the mountain of evil that Christians perpetrated?' Roger retorted.

'From my reading of history, the world was in a much worse state in the hands of Christians than it is now. The world actually became a better, more civilised place in the 20th century when the importance of Christianity began to diminish.'

'But the 20th century was the bloodiest, most murderous century in human history,' Sean pointed out. 'You mentioned the Crusades and the Spanish Inquisition? The numbers who died by their hands pale into insignificance compared to those wiped out by secular atheist governments in the 20th century. The communists in Russia, China and elsewhere wiped out millions upon millions of their own citizens who were deemed a threat to their plan of creating an equal, utopian society, free from the "bonds" of religion. Throughout its 2,000-year history, more Christians were put to death by secular atheist regimes in the 20th century than in all the other centuries put together – fact!'

'I didn't know that,' said a surprised Paul.

'Well, it's true,' said Sean. 'And today people like to focus on the negative aspects of Christian history, but they ignore all the good. They forget that Western civilisation has its roots in Christianity. Western civility and common decency, which we now take for granted, came from Christianity. This civility and common decency is still just about intact in the current era, but it's ebbing away with each generation as secularism increases its influence. You only have to ask an elderly person how things have changed. They'll tell you that fifty years ago people were more courteous, had more respect for one another, and just generally there was more of a respect for human dignity back then. But we're gradually losing this.'

'I don't buy that,' said Roger. 'Every generation thinks that things were better in the "good old days". People always look at the past through rose-tinted spectacles.'

'But society will grow colder, more cynical and more vulgar as Christian civility diminishes,' Sean asserted. 'If things continue as they're going, what we'll see is a full-blown return to pagan morals and values. But this post-Christian form of paganism will be even more far removed from Christianity than the original paganism. At least some of the original pagans, especially the ancient Greeks, were searching for God and were open to receiving spiritual truth. But the new paganism isn't interested in spiritual truth. It's built upon a rejection of Jesus Christ – who is the source of all truth. So it's anti-Christian in its nature because it kicks against what has come before, looking to replace the old moral order with a new order that's in many ways opposite it. The new paganism, as it exists now, revolves around the worship of science and nature, and won't accept any authority above the human intellect. It frighteningly sees the human being as nothing more than an highly evolved mammal with no ultimate purpose. In fact, when narrowed down, a human being is ultimately just a purposeless collection of atoms created accidentally by evolution. If there is such a thing as human love, that too only came to exist by genetic or evolutionary processes to aid the survival of the species. This crazy perception of who we are completely takes away our inherent worth as human beings. That's why the new pagan order will have no regard for the worth of human life. So brace yourself for very, very nasty times ahead.'

Roger shook his head and grinned.

'Again, I think you're going way over the top and being overdramatic,' he said. 'I honestly don't think the world is deteriorating like you think it is. You mentioned things being better fifty years ago? Well, I for one wouldn't want to have lived fifty years ago. Things were so staid and stuffy back then. I'll take this free and liberated era we're living in now, thank you very much. What do you think, Paul?'

Paul had a brief think.

'Erm… yeah, I agree,' he tentatively replied

An exasperated Sean decided not to respond, and he disconsolately reached for his mineral water. It seemed there was just no way of getting through to Roger.

11

The Inversion of Morals

Guided by Roger, the three of them took a jaunt to a traditional Dutch beer hall called Werner's, situated in Amsterdam's Jordaan district. Many Amsterdam natives could be found in this drinking establishment, although there were a few Brits in as well. A traditional Dutch drinking song could be heard in the background, adding to the distinctly Dutch atmosphere. Roger and Paul treated themselves to glasses of Dutch lager, whilst Sean stayed on water. They found a table for themselves and Roger got going again with his debate with Sean.

'Y'know, Sean, despite everything you've said, I still say no one has the right to impose his religion or morals onto someone else. That's why I firmly believe that religion has to be kept out of politics, out of education, out of our media. I accept that atheist, communist regimes went too far and impeded people's rights, but that didn't happen in the West. In the West we got the balance right. We learned to keep religion out of state and public affairs, while at the same time we respected people's religious liberties, and we ended up with a much more democratic society than we ever had before.'

Sean let out a laugh at Roger's naivety.

'This idea that we're living in a fair democracy is a myth,' he asserted; 'it's a façade, an illusion. The West is indirectly under the control of those who run big business and finance – it is they who are pulling all the strings. They might work through mediums such as the United Nations or the European Union, but ultimately it is *they* who have most of the world's nations in their pocket.'

'D'you reckon?' said Roger, predictably sceptical.

'Aye,' said Sean. 'Let's look at the UK as an example. In the UK we have two main political parties that dominate – one that claims to be conservative, the other socialist. But whichever one gets into power is at the mercy of those who control the world economy, i.e., the world banks. The world banks control the global flow of capital and the money supply and, like I've said, when you control the money supply you have great leverage to control everything else. And these world banks are *privately owned*, not government-owned –

they're run by sixty to eighty families – but you won't hear any of this on the news. And these people who control the world economy are materialists to the core. They reject God and worship money and power.'

'Sorry, Sean, but this again all sounds like paranoid-conspiracy-theory stuff,' Roger responded.

'It's not a theory, it's a fact,' Sean answered back. 'The whole world financial system is corrupt – it's effectively in the hands of crooks – but you won't hear this on the news either. The whole modern-day monetary system is corrupt. What modern banks are allowed to do is digitally create money that isn't backed by anything – in other words, it's money made up out of thin air. They then loan this fake money out and collect interest on the loans, thereby amassing wealth by totally fraudulent means. On top of that, these banking cartels have the power to shrink the money supply whenever they feel like it, creating boom and bust cycles, which result in companies going bust and having their assets – which have actual value – taken over by the banks. By these methods the banks accumulate more and more power, and with that power more and more control of our world. They use these completely unjust ways of amassing wealth, and there's a word for it… theft!'

Sean then took a sip of mineral water before saying more.

'Y'know, when you study history you'll always find that nations that were financially corrupt at the top always became immoral in everything else. This was the case in Sodom and in Babylon, and our world is effectively turning into one big Sodom. Because material greed and the lust for power is rooted in selfish impulses, and rebels against the natural law, a general breakdown of ethics and morals will always accompany it. This is why societies built on material greed always become selfish, pleasure-driven and sexually immoral; you'll always end up with a society governed by abnormal passions and appetites as opposed to reason.'

'So, what's the answer to the problem of capitalist greed and the desire for world domination?' asked Roger. 'Communism?'

Sean shook his head.

'Communism and liberal capitalism are opposite sides of the same coin,' he answered. 'They're evil twins, both deriving from the same source. One system makes you a slave to the state, the other makes you a slave to big business. Both communism and liberal capitalism result in wealth and labour being creamed off the masses and concentrated into the hands of the few. But if anything, communism is the more unjust system because it denies individual property rights and takes by force all it can for the state.'

Paul raised an eyebrow.

'I've never heard that before,' he said.

'Well, it's true,' said Sean. 'Most people don't know that the Russian Revolution was financed by Western banks. The banking oligarchs in the West supported communism in Russia for two reasons.

Firstly, they wanted a monopoly on world trade; the more communism was spread among the nations, the less competition there would be to challenge them. Secondly, the spreading of communism was the perfect way to bring about the emergence of a one-world government and a one-world economic system made up of lots of passive, state-controlled nations which they, the banking elite, would have total control of.'

Sean took a sip of his water before saying more.

'Communism was originally an idea of the West that was later refined and played out in the East. It derived from the ideas of the German philosophers, Karl Marx and Friedrich Engels, but was further developed by the likes of Lenin and Trotsky, and it became an experiment played out on the lives of hundreds of millions of poor Russians. What isn't always realised is that communism is a system which is completely materialist. Communists completely deny God and the supernatural. They believe that the only thing that exists is matter. A human being is nothing more than matter, nothing more than a collection of atoms, and therefore has no inherent worth. In the communist system, the state is everything, the state is God. A person's value or worth is measured by how much use he is to the state. A person must be of use to the collective, to the communal, to the state, otherwise he's of no worth. This is why it became so easy for communist regimes to wipe out all those millions who wouldn't co-operate with them. Killing humans came as easy to them as swatting flies.'

Roger and Paul remained silent, pondering on Sean's words. Then Sean had more to say.

'For most of the past century we've seen secular liberalism dominate in the West and communism dominate in the East. But liberals in the West have always been open to embracing communist or Marxist ideas. The common thread between secular liberalism and Marxism is that they both want to see society "de-Christianised" and both are determined that the Church can have no influence over the state. Both place *man* at the centre of all things as opposed to God. Both deny the existence of a natural law or natural order ordained by God, and flowing on from that they both have contempt for the very natural institutions of marriage and the family. Secular liberals have no great love for the family because they don't want to be bound by the responsibility of family life – it gets in the way of freedom and pleasure. Marxists want the institution of the family to be as weak as possible because the weaker the family is, the more control and influence the state can have over society. This is why both liberals and Marxists support feminism, sexual liberation, abortion rights, gay rights, transgender ideology, etc., because these things are all detrimental to the institutions of marriage and the family.'

Sean then gathered himself for a little think. He actually believed that the great architect behind the forces of secularism in all its guises was the devil himself. He believed that liberals, Marxists, humanists, gay rights activists, feminists, pro-abortionists, and all other groups at enmity with the Church, were all unknowingly allowing Satan to work through them and were all contributing to the establishment of a Satanic new world order where eventually the Antichrist would reign. But he didn't want to say all this to Roger and Paul. However, he did have more to say about the corruption of morals.

'What we see with the modern secular world is not just a corruption of morals but in some cases a complete inversion of morals. Things that common sense tell us are plainly immoral and wicked, such as abortion and pornography, are passed off as good, and things that common sense tell us are good and right are now presented to us as bad. We now get things pushed onto us that completely attack common sense – common sense that the average man in the street innately understands – and they try to pass it off as normal and acceptable.'

'But we're going round in circles,' Roger retorted. 'I've already said, no one has the right to dictate to us what is right and wrong, what is good and bad – including your Catholic Church! The Catholic Church has no more right to impose its morals on us than the liberals or Marxists. And all this stuff you're coming out with isn't twisting my arm or changing my mind about anything. I'm still a broad-minded liberal and a hedonist. After we leave this place, myself and Paul are heading right into the red-light district. We're gonna be smoking joints, going into sex shops to look at porno magazines, and then we'll be exploring the brothels to eye up the prostitutes, before ending the night at a sex club – and we're gonna have a whale of a time! I've said it once and I'll say it again – life is pointless without fun and pleasure. Only pleasure makes life worth living, and I'm sorry for anyone who doesn't realise that reality. What do you say, Paul?'

Paul had a brief think.

'Erm… yeah,' he tentatively replied.

For the rest of their stay in the beer hall, a frustrated Sean remained subdued and quiet. It seemed all the effort he was making to try and enlighten Roger and Paul in Christian truth was coming to nought. Eventually they left the beer hall, with a disheartened Sean going his own way for the rest of the night, whilst Roger and Paul headed back to the red-light zone.

12

The Human Zoo

A discouraged Sean went back to the hotel, frustrated at not making much headway in his efforts to lift Roger and Paul out of their darkness and draw them closer to the light. They just wouldn't take in and absorb his words, especially Roger. Meanwhile, Roger and Paul headed right into the heart of the red-light area. It seemed that none of what Sean had said had dissuaded them from indulging in seedy activity.

It was around 10pm. The red-light zone seemed to be engulfed by British tourists. In the midst of so many fellow Brits, Roger and Paul were very slowly walking along Warmoesstraat, one of the main streets of the red-light district, viewing the prostitutes. Roger was looking for one "lucky lady" whom he could spend his money on.

To cater for everyone's tastes, the prostitutes were loosely separated and compartmentalised into different zones within the area. The women were separated by nationality, race, hair colour, age, shape and size, etc. One area had predominantly blondes, another brunettes, and in other sections there could be found black women, Orientals, East Europeans, Latinos, chubby women, mature women, etc. Like goods in retail shop windows were these various women put on display. And various groups of mostly alcohol-filled men could be seen observing, pointing and laughing at what was on show around this human zoo.

There were several groups of British lads walking around, many on stag party weekends. They all seemed to dress the same way, whether they were from Liverpool, Manchester, London or Glasgow. Most of them were in long-sleeved shirts, stay-press trousers and black shoes – the same kind of attire they'd wear on a Friday or Saturday night back home. Roger and Paul were dressed in a similar fashion and thus blended right in with their compatriots. And something else they had in common was their unreserved ogling of the many women on display in the brothel windows.

'Have you found a babe that's taken your eye yet?' Paul asked Roger as they continued to slowly walk and look around.

'I've seen a couple of good ones but I haven't made my mind up yet,' answered Roger. 'I need to properly explore every nook and cranny before I finally choose my prize-winning wench.'

Paul laughed.

'What about you?' Roger asked. 'Don't you wanna dip into this feast of womanhood on offer?'

'I… I don't know,' Paul tentatively replied.

'Go on, be a devil,' Roger coaxed. 'We're in Amsterdam, for goodness sake. Just cut loose and indulge yourself while you're here.'

Paul stayed quiet. He wouldn't admit it, but all the religious talk from Sean had made him apprehensive of taking things too far.

As they continued to walk, Roger's bladder was feeling the effects of all his drinking.

'I badly need a urinal,' he informed Paul. 'I'm bursting. I just need to nip in to that pub on the corner to use their washroom. D'you need to go?'

'No, I'm alright,' replied Paul. 'I went before we left Werner's.'

They crossed the road and headed towards the pub on the corner of a side street. As Roger went in to the pub to relieve himself, Paul remained outside.

As Paul waited, he began to ponder on the idea of visiting a brothel. Half of him was keen, whilst the other half was saying "no way!". His attention was then drawn towards the brothels a little further down this side street. A curiosity came over him and he decided to walk a few steps down the street to investigate.

All the women on this particular street looked well past the age of forty, indicating that this was the mature ladies' section. Paul didn't find any of the women especially attractive, but one middle-aged lady caught his eye. She was the only one sitting down on the edge of her bed, not bothering to display herself in the window. The others were standing in their "shop" windows, all beady-eyed and eagerly seeking out potential customers. However, this one very sad-looking woman – whose short, dyed, auburn hair didn't stop her looking over the age of fifty – sat disconsolately on her bed, staring down at the floor while holding a cigarette. She seemed oblivious to what was going on outside of her four walls; almost locked in her own little world of woe. She had the saddest of eyes, and her lips were curved downwards in a permanent grimace. It was obvious she didn't get too many customers, and it was clear from her body language that her self-esteem had hit rock bottom.

Paul decided to cross the road to get a closer look. He approached the woman's window, yet still she wouldn't raise her head to take notice of someone. She continued to just sit and stare down at the carpet, cigarette in hand. A feeling of compassion stirred up inside Paul as he observed this woman, who looked clinically depressed. The sight of her brought home to Paul the reality that Amsterdam's prostitutes were real people leading real lives and not just images or emotionless objects in shop windows.

Paul turned from the woman's window and walked away across the street. As he walked back to the pub, he turned his head once more and from a distance saw the woman in exactly the same pose, sitting almost motionlessly on her bed, staring down at the floor.

Roger then emerged from the pub, feeling better for using its washroom facility.

'Ah, that's better!' he said. 'I needed that. Are you ready to resume our babe hunt?'

Paul was briefly silent.

'Yeah,' he eventually said, half-heartedly.

The two of them continued to walk around and meticulously explore the main streets and canals of De Wallen. They walked up and down Sint Annenstraat, Sint Jansstraat, Damstraat, Oudezijds Voorburgwal and Oudezijds Achterburgwal. Much to Paul's amusement, whenever Roger stopped at a prostitute's window, he seemed to instinctively pump out his chest muscles to try to impress her with his physique. And they continued this ambling around until Roger at last found his dream girl at the blondes section on the Oudezijds Achterburgwal. The young woman in question was a slim, tallish, pretty blonde. She stood exhibiting herself in the window, maintaining a confident, even arrogant, pose. She was undeniably blessed with beauty and she knew it. For Roger, she ticked all the right boxes in terms of physical attractiveness. She was certainly getting the most visual attention from the many groups of men passing her window.

'She's the one!' Roger told Paul, excitedly. 'She's most definitely the one! What d'you think?'

'Yeah, she's pretty,' Paul agreed. 'But I'm not really into blondes. I'm more of a brunettes man.'

'Ah, come on, Paul!' said a disbelieving Roger. 'Are you telling me you'd turn someone like that down?'

'No,' said Paul. 'I agree she's pretty, but she's just not my type. We all have our own tastes.'

'She is delectable!' said Roger, overcome with lust. 'I mean, look at her. Look at all these fellas eyeing her up. She's outta this world; an angel!'

'Is she your choice, then?' Paul asked.

'Well, we're not gonna meet anyone better than her, are we?' answered Roger.

'So, are you going to pay her a visit tonight?' Paul asked.

'I need to find out how much she charges,' replied Roger. 'She might charge a bit more than the going rate cos she's extra gorgeous.'

'Well, knock on her door and find out,' Paul advised him.

With little hesitation, Roger went and did exactly that. A taken-aback Paul watched on as Roger was greeted at the door by the beautiful blonde and began exchanging words with her.

Roger discovered by her accent that the woman was Dutch, and she didn't charge any more than the usual rates for her services. After discovering her prices, he told her she'd receive a visit from him the following night.

Paul then saw the prostitute shut her door and Roger walk back to him with an excited, yet nervous, demeanour about him.

'What happened?' Paul asked.

'I'm going to see her tomorrow night,' said Roger.

'Why not tonight?' a curious Paul asked. 'Haven't you got enough money on you?'

'Yeah, I've got more than enough,' said Roger. 'It's just that I'm a bit over-excited and nervous. I need to calm down a bit. I'll be mentally more prepared tomorrow night.'

Paul couldn't help but laugh.

'Come on, let's find a coffee shop,' Roger then proposed. 'I need to puff on a nice, soothing, relaxing joint to calm down all this excitement that's rippling through me.'

Roger and Paul then headed to a coffee shop for a smoke. After that they spent most of the rest of the night repeating a routine of drinking, smoking joints and visiting sex shops. They ended the night watching an erotic cabaret show at a club Roger knew well. They finally staggered back to their hotel at around 3am.

13

A Gift That's Not Cheap

It was Saturday afternoon – the second day of the trip. Sean was walking along the Damrak. With just a street map and guide for company, he'd spent the early part of the day on his own, exploring the city. He'd visited the Anne Frank House, the Rijksmuseum (Amsterdam's biggest art museum), and he'd visited the Van Gogh Museum to look at the work of a now world-famous artist who died penniless. He'd agreed to meet up with Roger and Paul at Jack's Bar, an American-style bar situated on the Damrak.

It was pretty difficult not to notice Jack's Bar, as its name was lit up in huge, neon red letters, and it was always a hive of noise and activity from noon until night. Sean entered the crowded establishment and was greeted to the sight of several waitresses all wearing bright pink shorts, and white T-shirts with the words "Jack's Bar" printed across them. Sean spotted Roger and Paul, who in turn spotted him and signalled him over to their table. Resting on their table sat a great, bulky, glass jug of American lager. It seemed that the amount of drink they'd had the previous day hadn't put them off getting tanked up all over again.

'Sean, my good man, pull up a chair,' a tipsy Roger greeted him.

'What have you been doing with yourself?' Paul asked.

'Oh, this and that,' said Sean. 'I toured around. I went to the Anne Frank House and the Van Gogh Museum, and other places.'

'How enormously exciting!' Roger said in mocking jest. 'What a positively stimulating time you must have had. But forget the art of Van Gogh, look at all the gorgeous works of art around here. Wouldn't you like to get a load of beer down you and try to pull one of them?'

Sean looked around and observed some of the "gorgeous works of art" Roger was talking about. He had to admit that all the waitresses were pretty – or else they probably wouldn't be employed there. He especially took notice of one of the girls vainly looking into a mirrored wall beside the bar. She was fixing the front of her hair with her fingers, and while doing so was taking a long, lingering look at her own pretty face.

'Admiring one of the girls?' Paul asked Sean, breaking his observation.

'No, I'm watching her admire herself in the mirror,' Sean replied.

'What a body she's got, though,' said Roger. 'Almost as good as that angelic blonde I'm gonna to be seeing tonight.'

Sean indented his eyebrows in confusion.

'What angelic blonde is that?' he asked.

'He's having his wicked way with a stunning Dutch blonde in the red-light district tonight,' Paul informed Sean.

Sean was briefly stunned.

'You're really going through with it?' he asked Roger.

'I sure am,' Roger unashamedly replied.

Sean was caught in a quandary. Should he keep his mouth shut and mind his own business, or should he do all he could to dissuade Roger from participating in such an act? He decided to listen to his conscience.

'Y'know, I wouldn't be much of a Christian if I didn't warn you of the serious sin you'll be committing,' he bravely told Roger.

Roger smirked and rolled his eyes before replying.

'What is sinful about two consenting adults having a bit of fun together?'

Sean smiled wryly at Roger's lack of scruples.

'Sex between a man and a woman is much, much more than just a bit of fun,' he answered back.

'Well, that's not how I see it,' said Roger. 'I know you Christians think that sex is dirty, but the rest of the world sees it for what it really is – one of life's great pleasures, to be celebrated and indulged in. And that's just what I'm gonna be doing tonight.'

'I don't think of sex as something dirty,' Sean told Roger. 'It is God who created sexual pleasure and everything created by Him was good. But He gave us this gift to be enjoyed only under certain conditions.'

'And what conditions are those?' asked Roger.

'Within the bounds of a fully committed relationship between a husband and wife who are open to creating new life,' Sean replied.

A befuddled Roger shook his head.

'Why?' he asked.

'The act of sex can only take place within the bounds of marriage, where a man and woman have fully committed themselves to one another for life,' said Sean. 'And as I said, they must be open to creating new life. But we're now living in a culture that tries to separate sex from procreation, reducing the sexual act to nothing more than a leisure activity.'

Roger sternly shook his head before responding.

'What is so wrong about two people enjoying sex just for the pleasure of it? And what exactly is wrong with enjoying it as a leisure activity? Why do Christians have such a problem with that?'

'The sexual act should be all about a husband and wife offering themselves to one another completely in a physical and spiritual act of love,' Sean explained. 'And the ultimate motive of the act must be the creation of new life, in co-operation with whatever God wills – so that rules out any form of contraception. When a married couple enjoys sex in this natural way it receives God's blessing and it becomes a very pure and even holy act. But if sexual activity takes place in any other way the act becomes defiled and no longer has God's blessing behind it.'

'Are you telling me that in order for a couple to have a good, long-term sex life they have to be prepared to have child after child after child?' Roger questioned. 'So they end up with a small army of kids to take care of?'

'When a couple are not prepared to have children they must simply abstain from sex,' said Sean. 'The ultimate purpose of sex is to create new life, just as the ultimate purpose of eating is to keep us alive. The pleasures that come with sex or with eating are wonderful God-given bonuses, but they must never be treated as ends in themselves.'

'No offence, Sean, but what a load of codswallop!' said Roger. 'Sorry, but I just cannot logically see why we can't enjoy sex for the sheer fun of it. And what is all this nonsense about it being a sacred, spiritual act? I agree that the ultimate purpose of sex is to procreate, but I see no reason why we can't unreservedly feast on the pleasure it gives. And I see no reason why we have to attach any love or life-long commitment with it. The sexual drive is a pure, animalistic drive – like the need to eat. There's absolutely nothing spiritual about it.'

'You're wrong,' said Sean. 'There is a spiritual element to sex. There's also an element of mystery attached to our sexuality. That's the way God created it. Our sexuality is a precious, extremely personal gift that cannot be given away cheaply. Why do you think rape or sexual abuse has such a damaging effect on a person? It does so much damage precisely because our sexuality is something so precious and personal.'

There was momentary silence at the table as Roger and Paul tried to digest what Sean was saying. Then Sean had more to say.

'As I've said, sex can only be enjoyed within the bounds of marriage and under the conditions I've just described – and not in any other way! There's no room for contraception or fornication or adultery or homosexual acts or masturbation. These things all violate God's natural law in a very serious way.'

Roger indented his eyebrows.

'Even masturbation?' he questioned.

'Aye, even masturbation,' answered Sean.

'Why?' a bemused Roger asked. 'I mean, what harm are you doing anyone?'

'You're harming yourself,' said Sean.

'How?' Paul asked.

'Again, because you're taking sex out of its proper context and cheapening it,' replied Sean. 'Masturbation

114

is an activity that's very inward and self-centred – that's why it offends God.'

Roger scratched his head in bewilderment before responding.

'Surely if you're not regularly having sex with a partner, and you don't masturbate, there's gonna be a build-up of sperm, isn't there? In the end you have to somehow get rid of it.'

'No,' said Sean, 'that's a myth. Medical research shows that when a man abstains from sexual activity any sperm he's produced dies and gets recycled back into the body. So, no unhealthy build-up of sperm ever takes place.'

Roger was briefly silent. He'd never heard this before.

'But surely a man's sex drive needs to be satisfied, doesn't it?' he argued. 'Surely a man would go out of his head if he didn't regularly relieve himself? I know I would.'

'What you're saying might be the case for someone who's addicted or regularly indulges in the habit, because the body and mind are so used to it,' Sean answered. 'But for someone who consciously abstains from it and, by God's grace, manages to keep out sexual or lustful thoughts, it's possible to keep the sex drive well in check. The key to it is avoiding stimulation by keeping sexual or lustful thoughts at bay. We can't do that on our own because both the devil and our own sinful nature are too powerful for us. We can only manage it by turning to God and praying for the grace to overcome it.'

'What's so wrong about lust?' Roger then asked with bemusement. 'Surely lust is perfectly natural and normal? We all have lustful thoughts – even priests. Surely the sex drive is driven by lust?'

'Most people don't properly understand what the word "lust" means,' said Sean. 'Lust revolves around objectifying another person for your own pleasure. When you look at someone in a lustful way you're no longer looking at or respecting them as a whole person but reducing them to how much sexual stimulation they can provide you with. You're reducing them to a thing, not a person. You're using them. So, lust by its very nature is selfish and self-centred and in opposition to love. This is a major reason why pornography is so harmful – it encourages us to look at human beings as objects, not complete persons. Pornography de-humanises people.'

While Roger and Paul were quietly mulling over Sean's words, a waitress came over to their table. The pretty young blonde had noticed that Sean wasn't drinking and that prompted her to their table. She was also enticed by Sean's handsome looks.

'Hello, boys,' she greeted them in a Dutch accent. 'Can I get you anything?'

Roger and Paul declined as they still had half a jug of lager to finish, but Sean ordered a mineral water. When the waitress left to get Sean's drink, Roger began to letch over her, illustrating a scant regard for what Sean had just told him.

'Wow, what a body she's got,' he said, licking his lips. 'You're not going to stop me lusting over a babe like that!'

While Paul tittered, Sean shook his head, wondering whether it was worth saying any more.

'Anyway,' Roger then said to Sean, 'you say lust degrades the one on the receiving end, but most women want men to find them sexually attractive. I know some women who only live to tease and titillate men – it's their main pleasure in life. And look at all these waitresses. See how flirty they are, and the way they're flaunting themselves at the customers? They're loving all the looks and attention they're getting. This behaviour is perfectly natural. Women have to flaunt their sexuality to attract a mate. As for me, I personally wouldn't have any problems at all with any woman lusting over me. I'd have no objections if any woman wanted to look at me as a sexual object.'

'That's highly unlikely, isn't it?' said Paul with a cheeky smile on his face.

Roger gave Paul a look of scorn before turning back to Sean to speak.

'Y'know, we went to a live sex show last night where we saw several women taking their clothes off and exhibiting themselves on stage, and you could tell they weren't just doing their job for the money. They were more than happy to be there. They thoroughly enjoyed the attention they were getting, and we enjoyed looking. The enjoyment was mutual. So where's the harm being done?'

'Women who resort to using their sexuality to attract the attention of men tend to be very lonely on the inside,' Sean put forward. 'And they tend to have distorted views of what love is. They think they're receiving a type of love when they stir men's passions, but really they're getting nothing. Those women you saw yesterday at that club may have enjoyed the attention they were getting, but in reality all they were getting was lots of men objectifying them and using them for their own pleasure. Those women were getting lots of lust but no love. So, in some respects, they ended up receiving the very opposite of what they wanted, because in the eyes of the men gazing at them they were nothing more than "things" or objects to be used for titillation and amusement.'

At that moment, the pretty blonde waitress came back to the table with a mineral water for Sean. While she served and exchanged pleasantries, Roger was again lecherously eyeing her up and down. After she'd walked off he turned to Sean to speak again.

'I mean, look at that gorgeous babe! Are you seriously telling me you're not getting any thoughts or feelings of lust for a stunner like that?'

Sean shook his head in all sincerity.

'Well, you either must be gay or have lost your sex drive, mate,' said Roger.

'I'm not gay and my sexual drive remains in reserve,' Sean answered. 'I just try to respect every person's dignity. That waitress isn't a walking, talking sexual image. She's a real person. She's someone's daughter, perhaps someone's sister. You can't reduce a human being to an object or image.'

14

Sugar-coated Poison

The three of them remained inside Jack's Bar. Sean was keen to leave and go somewhere else, but Roger and Paul still had some of their jug of lager to finish. Roger continued to eye up the young ladies and pass comment.

'Fine-looking ladies like these make life worth living,' he said. 'Sorry, Sean, but women like these were made to be ogled and lusted over.'

Sean remained quiet. It seemed pointless to say any more on the subject of lust.

'I still think it's not natural for a man not to lust over a woman,' Roger continued. 'It's not healthy for a man to suppress his fleshly appetites. Our sexual drive has to have an outlet. I mean, I don't mean to offend you, but look at all those Catholic priests involved in sexual molestation. It must have something to do with them being sexually repressed, brought on by their vows of celibacy.'

Sean both smiled and grimaced at Roger's insinuation.

'Catholic priests do not become sexual molesters!' he then adamantly responded. 'It works the other way round. Sexual molesters become Catholic priests! Molesters become Catholic priests for the same reason they become teachers or social workers or health workers. The Catholic priesthood potentially offers a gateway, an access to the young and vulnerable, and that's why it attracts molesters. But I know from direct experience that the earnest practice of celibacy does not lead to unhealthy sexual repression or cause someone to become a sexual offender – that is a lie and a myth!'

'I wouldn't be so sure of that,' said an unconvinced Roger. 'I still say the sexual drive has to be relieved. That's why society needs pornography. There has to be some sort of outlet where a man can direct his natural, biological urges.'

An increasingly exasperated Sean briefly shut his eyes and scratched his forehead.

'Pornography can never deliver what it promises and always leaves a bitter aftertaste,' he answered. 'The problem with pornography is that the outer packaging is always far better than what's inside. It promises something good, but in the end it will always bring harm… like sugar-coated poison.'

'Well, I've been watching porno films and looking at magazines for years and it hasn't done me any harm,' Roger claimed.

'I'd like to think it hasn't done me any major harm, either,' Paul concurred.

Sean decided not to comment.

'And anyway, social research points out that porn actually benefits society,' said Roger. 'It satisfies a need. That's why countries that are sexually very open and where hardcore porn is legal, such as Holland and Denmark, have less cases of rape and sexual abuse than in religious countries where it's not legal. Statistics back this up. So how do you explain that?'

'I'd take those statistics with a pinch of salt,' said Sean. 'What you have to remember is that the porn industry is a multi-billion dollar industry that will influence facts and twist statistics to justify its existence. I guarantee you, in Western countries, where it's readily available, the vast majority of rapists and sexual offenders are heavily into pornography – and often it does play a part in them committing the offence.'

'So why do non-religious countries, where people aren't so repressed, have lower cases of rape?' Roger retorted.

'Don't you believe it!' Sean answered. 'The porn industry has the money and even political backing from liberals to set up these bogus commissions that allegedly do "honest" research into the effects of porn on society. But they're full of deception. According to other statisticians, in Denmark sexual crime has gone up by 300 per cent since porn became popular there in the late '60s. I would suggest those findings are more reliable. And so-called "soft" porn does just about the same damage as the hardcore stuff. It still leaves a person unsatisfied, hungry for more and sexually frustrated.'

'D'you reckon?' said Roger, disparagingly.

'Aye,' said Sean. 'The problem with pornography is that it can only arouse the passions but never satisfy them because it completely twists and perverts God's true purpose for human sexuality. It so contravenes God's natural law that by its very nature it can never satisfy or fulfil a person because the person who uses it automatically severs himself from God and therefore can't receive the true joy that can only come with His blessing and grace. Without His blessing and grace nothing good or worthwhile can come to a person.'

'Well, I personally couldn't live without porn!' said Roger. 'I just couldn't even begin to imagine life without it. So there must be something good about it.'

'But do you know that porn is addictive?' Sean responded. 'It's as addictive as any recreational drug. When we use pornography we innately know in our subconscious that what we're doing is wrong so, consequently, along with the hormones that come with sexual arousal, we simultaneously feel the effects of stress hormones that always come with negative emotions or feelings. And it's this unnatural intermingling of bodily hormones that make it addictive. The arousal that comes from watching porn can never be satisfied or fulfilled, and the person ends up with all these unwanted, biological secretions in his system which need getting rid of. This is why a man addicted to pornography will be prone to depression, stress, anger problems and even paranoia.'

Roger defiantly shook his head.

'Well, I wouldn't say I suffer from any terrible stress or depression,' he claimed. 'Nor do I suffer from any other emotional hang-up.'

'Are you sure about that?' said Sean.

'Yes,' said Roger after a brief think.

Sean, though, still had more to say.

'So much about the porn industry is kept hidden – like the fact that the industry draws and attracts a distinct type of young adult to work in it. So often, the young adults recruited into the industry tend to spring out of difficult, dysfunctional family backgrounds. They commonly come out of broken homes, brought up in unstable, unloving environments and so tend to be inflicted with very low self-worth and low self-esteem, and it's this lack of self-esteem and self-respect that make them so vulnerable to the manipulation and exploitation of the porn industry. And involvement in the industry makes their lives worse, not better.'

A smirking Roger remained sceptical, but Sean still had more to say.

'D'you know, in America, a chillingly high percentage of sex industry workers don't make it past the age of forty?' Sean explained. 'Due to the money they make, many of them get involved in hard drugs. They get into drugs because once the thrill of their sexual activity fades they need to seek out some other form of pleasure to substitute it with. Because they're so spiritually dead they become completely dependent on fleeting moments of pleasure and physical sensation to lift them out of their sad, empty lives. Some of them end up so psychologically messed up and disturbed that it eventually pushes them into topping themselves.'

'Are you sure all this is hard fact and not exaggeration?' said Roger.

'Pretty sure,' said Sean.

'You mentioned people being deceptive with facts and statistics, but are you sure it doesn't happen the other way?' Roger proposed. 'What makes you think the anti-porn brigade aren't twisting the truth for their own ends? Sorry, Sean, but nothing you're saying is putting me off porn or the sex industry. And I'm still visiting that brothel tonight.'

15

The Rock That's Crumbling

It had just gone 6pm and the three of them were back in Molly Malone's. The pub was again packed with Brits, generating an atmosphere reminding them of home. Roger and Paul had gone Irish and switched to stout, while Sean was content with a fruit juice. As they settled with their drinks, they resumed their conversation. Sean felt the need to say more on pornography and the breakdown of sexual ethics in the culture.

'Y'know, the legalisation of pornography and the rise of sexual permissiveness was always going to come once it became socially acceptable to separate the sexual act from its primary purpose. It was people like Sigmund Freud who pushed on us all these crazy new ideas about human sexuality, and unfortunately too many people took his ideas seriously. But the main catalyst for the breakdown of sexual ethics in society came with the popularisation of contraception.'

'Contraception?' Roger queried.

'Aye,' said Sean. 'If you study ancient history you'll find that all cultures that embraced unnatural means of birth control always, ultimately, went on to embrace "anything goes" sexual morals. When sex gets separated from procreation and is reduced to little more than a leisure activity, the sky's the limit. Anything and everything eventually becomes permissible, and boundaries will continue to be pushed.'

'I think you're getting a wee bit carried away again,' said Roger.

'I'm not,' answered Sean. 'When sex gets separated from what it was naturally intended for, absolutely any abnormal sexual practice can be justified and become accepted as normal. And, in my opinion, our society is becoming more and more permissive and more and more difficult to shock.'

Roger felt the need to firmly retort.

'Look, Sean, you go on and on about our society being permissive. So what? I still don't see why that's such a terrible thing. Why have you got such a hang-up about it? Why are you so threatened by it?'

'You're right, I do feel threatened by it,' said Sean. 'We all should.'

'Why?' asked Roger.

'Because sexual permissiveness threatens the institution of marriage and the family, and so threatens society at large,' Sean explained. 'The family as an institution is deteriorating because fornication and adulterous behaviour is now rife. Sexual permissiveness wrecks family life, and when the family goes, society goes with it. The strength of society is built upon the strength of the family. The family is the *rock*, the foundation that a strong nation is built upon. Remove or weaken this rock and everything else crumbles with it. And without a doubt the sexualising of our culture has given birth to an adulterous generation that no longer wants to take seriously the sanctity of marriage or uphold the family as the essential institution that it is.'

'D'you reckon?' said Roger, again disdainful.

'Aye,' Sean replied. 'And historical evidence backs me up. Ancient cultures that drifted into sexual permissiveness always fell into ruin. They all crumbled. Few more so than God's chosen people in Israel. But then you can look at ancient Rome or Greece or India. Whenever ancient societies descended into sexual immorality they always eventually self-destructed. It was through trial and error that these societies came to recognise the virtues of abstinence and temperance, and they came to recognise the importance of fidelity in marriage and maintaining the strength of the family.'

'Sorry, Sean, but I completely disagree,' said Roger. 'The sexualising of our culture just hasn't had the terrible effect on us that you're making out. In fact, since its liberation from biblical morals, the Western world has far from collapsed; if anything, it's gone from strength to strength. The West is still powerful and strong. What you say just doesn't stand up.'

'The West has morally and spiritually deteriorated and unless it turns away from this path will pay the consequences for it,' Sean adamantly replied. 'The ancient city of Sodom wasn't punished straight away for its immorality. That decadent city was allowed to grow in prosperity and power before God finally struck it down. God struck down Sodom for its material greed and its sexual immorality – the very two things that are now plaguing the modern Western world. A few centuries later, the city of Babylon was destroyed for similar reasons, never to recover.'

'But you can't compare ancient Rome or Babylon or Sodom with the modern Western world,' Roger argued. 'Those cities and those times were completely unjust and inhumane. We're socially a lot more advanced and civilised than they were. We're definitely more humane than they ever were.'

Sean again shook his head.

'In our own way, we're every bit as unjust and inhumane as them,' he countered. 'The difference is that the inhumanity of today is much more subtle and disguised – it's not as obvious and flagrant as it used to be. Because we're still living in a post-Christian age where Christian civility and decency still persists to a degree, today's inhumanity has to be dressed up and somehow made acceptable through very clever and cunning persuasion. But as I've said, the greatest genocide in human history is taking place right now in this era you're claiming to be so civilised and humane.'

'You're talking about abortion?' said Paul.

'Aye,' said Sean.

'I think genocide is a bit of a strong word when you're talking about abortion,' said Roger.

'No it isn't,' Sean replied. 'Abortion is the deliberate taking of an innocent life in the womb. And since abortion was first legalised in the 20th century, hundreds of millions of unborn babies have been wiped out, worldwide. So it's fair to describe it as a holocaust or genocide.'

Both Roger and Paul silently reached for their pints of stout, so Sean continued.

'There are also those countless deaths caused by the use of both the contraceptive pill and the morning-after pill, both of which can cause the discharge of an embryo, thus killing an unborn human.'

There was a brief silence. Then Roger gave his opinion.

'For the most part, I'm against abortion,' he said. 'The only time I think it might be justified is when an unborn kid is known to have something wrong with it. If they know the kid will be severely handicapped in some way, then I think abortion might be justified. I mean, why bring a child into the world only for it to suffer with a handicap all its life?'

'Human life is sacred and precious and it belongs to God,' Sean replied. 'It's not for us to decide who should live and who should die. We can't treat human life like factory toys where we get rid of the ones that have faults. In the eyes of God, a handicapped child is every bit as precious as an able-bodied child.'

Roger remained silent and reached for his stout again, so Sean continued.

'As I've said, because we've become such an atheistic and materialistic society, we've lost respect for the inherent worth of human beings and the sacredness of human life. If, at the end of the day, the human being is nothing more than a walking, talking clump of cells, created by accident and without any purpose, why not treat people as objects or things to be used or thrown away?'

Sean then paused for thought before saying more.

'I don't want to sound like a parrot, repeating myself, but what really triggered off this modern-day plague of abortion was the popularisation of contraception.'

Roger rolled his eyes.

'That again?' he said.

'Aye, that again,' said Sean. 'The popularisation of contraception saw people wanting the pleasure out of sex without the consequences, and that led to an eventual tolerance for abortion. And the Catholic

Church predicted some sixty years ago that the widespread use of contraception would eventually lead to the legalisation of abortion, and abortion, in turn, would eventually lead to euthanasia. For 2,000 years, the Church has been against unnatural means of birth control because societies that tolerate it will always go on to tolerate abortion. And now most of what the Church predicted has come to pass. Contraception did lead to abortion, and abortion has led to euthanasia. Voluntary euthanasia is legal here in Holland, and more countries are following suit. And the way things are going, in my opinion, it's only a matter of time before involuntary or forced euthanasia will be implemented on all those who are seen to be a burden on society, such as the long-term sick and the elderly. There could even come a time when infanticide – that's the killing of children who have been born – will become legal.'

'Ah, come on,' said Roger. 'That's never gonna happen.'

'Unless we do all we can to stop this abortion epidemic that will be the final outcome,' Sean warned. 'The acceptance of abortion equates with a complete disregard for the sacredness of human life and human worth. It justifies the taking of innocent lives. And God will not allow this to continue for too long. There will be a reckoning. A great chastisement will come upon humanity for allowing this to happen.'

16

Love and Sacrifice

The three of them had left Molly Malone's and were now back in Mae Wong's for supper. In the midst of their eating, they continued with the same heavy discussion that had engaged them in the pub.

'As I said before, I'm actually not completely against abortion,' said Roger. 'I think in the case of babies known to have deformities or handicaps it's perfectly reasonable for a mother to terminate the pregnancy. That saves a lot of suffering for all involved.'

'I agree,' Paul concurred.

'But if God allows a baby to be born with severe disabilities He must have good reasons for it,' said Sean. 'God allows suffering on this earth for His purposes – because only He can see the bigger picture. But we're now living in a culture where people want to avoid suffering at all costs. There's no focus on eternity, only the here and now. Therefore, earthly pleasures and comforts have become the be all and end all of life. This lies at the heart of the abortion epidemic. Women are told that babies are too much of a burden – they require too much time and sacrifice. They're told that a baby will mess up their life, ruin their career and get in the way of their fun and enjoyment. They're told that the very thing they're most naturally equipped for – motherhood – is bad for them.'

While Roger and Paul chewed on their chow mein, Sean expanded on his words.

'The problem is that we've lost the spirit of sacrifice. We want instant gratification; and that's given birth to a culture of selfishness, where we seek to lead lives free from suffering and discomfort. But in a broken world, full of people in need, it's impossible to love others without suffering ourselves, without a spirit of sacrifice. This is why modern society has become so apathetic and without love – people just don't want to lead selfless, sacrificial lives. Even most modern-day Christians have lost the spirit of sacrifice. They want Christianity without the cross. They're happy to receive the fruits of Christ's sacrifice on the cross but don't want to participate in the work of the cross as He called us to.'

Then Paul had something to say.

'I must admit, even though I was brought up a Catholic I've never fully understood Christ's sacrifice on the cross. I've never understood how one man's suffering can make amends for the sins of another. How does that work?'

Before Sean could reply, Roger interjected with his opinions.

'This idea that Jesus died for our sins makes no sense. There's no logic behind it. No offence, but how on earth can my sins be atoned for by a man put to death 2,000 years ago?'

Sean quickly swallowed down what was in his mouth. He had briefly touched on the subject of Christ's atonement the day before but was pleased for the opportunity to more fully explain to Roger and Paul the meaning of Christ's death on the cross, to explain to them the whole crux of his faith. However, he also had some apprehensions because so often people struggled to grasp it. He sipped some mineral water and then made an attempt to explain.

'No one can really understand Christ's death on the cross unless they can comprehend and realise the seriousness of sin. Sin – that is the breaking of God's laws – separated us from God and brought suffering and death into the world. As I said yesterday, all of us are born with the curse of original sin, a curse which we genetically inherit. This means we're all born with a sinful nature, with an inclination to rebel against God and do wrong. We carry around with us this sinful nature, resulting in us being stained by personal sin. Unless we are cleansed, we're all damned to hell. What must be realised is that God cannot tolerate sin, otherwise He wouldn't be God. Because of His complete goodness, His complete holiness and His perfect justice, it's impossible for Him to just let sins go. Therefore, in justice, a price must be paid. But because the sinfulness of man offended God in an infinite way, only a sacrifice of infinite worth would suffice to redeem man, and only God Himself was qualified to offer this sacrifice. This is why Jesus – who is God and infinitely perfect – came down to earth, becoming one of us, to offer Himself as a perfect, sinless, human sacrifice to appease the just wrath of God and purchase the grace to save mankind.'

Roger had a question.

'You say Jesus is God, but He's also the Son of God. How can He be both?'

'God is an entity of Three Persons,' answered Sean, 'made up of the Father, the Son and the Holy Spirit.'

'So it's three gods that you worship?' asked Roger.

'No,' said Sean, 'it's One God of Three Persons. The nature and essence of all Three are exactly the same. It's difficult for me to explain the Trinity without getting very deep and theological. I know on the surface it seems confusing.'

'Just a bit,' said Roger.

'The Holy Trinity is a mystery that we can never fully understand,' Sean admitted, 'but by faith all Christians accept the dogma.'

'So, I'll ask again,' said Roger, 'how does Jesus coming down to earth and dying on the cross make up for the sins of mankind? I'm still confused. Please explain it to me.'

Sean took another sip of his mineral water and then proceeded to answer.

'In the same way that it's impossible to understand the cross unless you understand the seriousness of sin, you also cannot understand the meaning of Christ's sacrifice unless you understand exactly what true love is. Christ's crucifixion represents the ultimate act of love. He loved us so much that He was prepared to come down to earth from heaven, become fully human like us, live a perfect life and offer Himself to God in atonement for our sins. His sacrifice not only purchased the grace to save every person from deserved damnation but also conquered death. As I said yesterday, death came into the world through sin. Christ, by His sacrifice, overcame the power of death, which was proved by His rising from the dead three days after His crucifixion.'

'But how does sacrifice – any sacrifice – make amends for sin?' asked Roger. 'I don't get it.'

'In God's law of justice, sacrifice is able to make amends for sin. God is appeased by sacrifice because sacrifice always involves denying yourself or dying to yourself. Sacrifice is the exact opposite of selfishness and self-indulgence – and all sin is essentially rooted in selfishness. So, in the same way that the fall of man came through an act of selfishness and pride, man's redemption came through an ultimate act of selflessness and love. Man was incapable of offering this sacrifice; only God in the person of a man, Jesus Christ, could offer this perfect sacrifice on man's behalf.'

Sean paused for thought before saying more.

'In so many ways, Christ's crucifixion was a reversal of the sin of Adam and Eve. For example, Adam and Eve were motivated by pride when they decided to defy God and eat the forbidden fruit, as the devil told them they would become gods themselves if they ate. Conversely, Christ's crucifixion showed a willingness to suffer great humiliation – as public crucifixion was one of the most humiliating and shameful ways to be put to death. Also, Adam and Eve were not able to mortify themselves against the temptation to eat the forbidden fruit, whereas Christ had to go through extreme mortification to fight the temptation to come down from the cross. And whilst Adam and Eve showed through their disobedience a lack of faith and trust in God, Christ demonstrated complete trust in God the Father by His perseverance unto death on the cross.'

'But where's the justice in allowing an innocent man to suffer for the sins of another?' asked Roger. 'It makes no sense.'

'It was the love of Christ that justified it,' Sean asserted. 'He chose to die for us out of pure love for us. And in the eyes of God, His act of love was more powerful than all of our acts of sin. But human beings still have free will, therefore Jesus will not force His saving grace on anyone. We are given the choice to follow Jesus or reject Him. We can only receive His gift of salvation when we are born again in Him through baptism and thereafter stay in communion with Him, which means following the sacraments of the only Church He established – the Catholic Church. We have to repent and be continually cleansed of sin, which means observing the sacrament of Confession, and we have to be nourished by the body and blood of Christ through the sacrament of Holy Communion. When we do this we become spiritually regenerated, paving the way to becoming new creations, to becoming like Jesus.'

Roger indented his eyebrows.

'What about all the people in the world who haven't been told about Jesus or the Catholic Church?' he said. 'Are they all damned?'

'No one can be saved independently from the saving grace of Jesus Christ,' Sean replied. 'But obviously there are people in the world who, through no fault of their own, know nothing about Jesus Christ or His Church. But God in His mercy still gives those who have never been told about Jesus the grace to be saved. A certain amount of grace and spiritual truth, such as having an innate sense of God's natural law, is given to all of us, including those with no knowledge of Jesus. It's down to the individual to follow their conscience and respond to this grace. We all have the free-will choice to either co-operate with the grace that comes to us or reject it. Therefore, on the Day of Judgement, no one will have an excuse. And obviously, anyone who comes into the knowledge of Jesus Christ and His teachings, as understood and explained by His Church, but chooses to reject Him has no excuse and will be damned.'

Sean paused, noticing a sober look on the face of Paul at his words. Then he continued.

'I also need to point out that only a saint can make it straight to heaven. All others will either end up in hell forever, or will have to go through a final purification, known as purgatory, before being admitted into heaven. But Christ gives all of us the grace to become saints; and it's important to understand how the system of grace works. Christ gives us grace – merited by His sacrifice on the cross – and then we have to make the free-will choice to co-operate with this grace. For those who respond to His grace, more grace will be given, allowing us to be moved towards holiness and sainthood. Conversely, if we make the free-will decision to reject Christ, He will respect that decision and withdraw from us. If we disown Him, He will disown us.'

Then Paul had a question.

'You said that anyone who follows Jesus will become like Him. What does that mean… to be like Jesus?'

'The nature of Jesus is pure love,' answered Sean. 'And He's not just a little bit loving, He's completely loving. His love is perfect. All Christians are called to follow His example of love.'

'But His love can't be that perfect if He sends anyone who refuses to accept Him into hell for all eternity!' Roger sniped. 'And what exactly is "love" anyway? I mean, is there even any such thing as love?'

'Aye, there is such a thing as love,' Sean answered. 'Love – real love – means valuing the needs and well-being of others as much as ourselves. In fact, Christ commands us to put others ahead of ourselves – that means being prepared to suffer and put yourself out for the benefit of others. Anyone who becomes a Christian is born again in Christ, is grafted into the life of Christ, and the life of Christ is a life of sacrifice. As I said yesterday, the Christian life is a life of sacrifice; that's why so many people find it difficult and stumble because of the inevitable suffering and discomfort involved in truly loving other people. But love equals sacrifice.'

17

Prophecies and Miracles

It had just gone 9pm and the three of them were back at the always crowded Saint George pub, sitting with their drinks and continuing their debate. Despite all Sean had told him, Roger was still unbending in his anti-Christian convictions. If anything, he'd grown more determined to prove Sean wrong.

'What gets me about Christians is how they assume themselves to be correct over all other faiths,' he complained. 'I know you said yesterday that you believe Jesus is God because you think He dwells within you and you've encountered Him, but I need more than that. Where's the objective evidence that God came down to earth in the person of Jesus? I'll accept that a man called Jesus once walked upon the earth, but where's the solid evidence that He was God in human form?'

'The miracles He performed and His rising from the dead are a good indication,' Sean argued.

'Where's the rock-hard evidence to back up all His supposed miracles or His rising from the dead?' queried Roger.

'Historical evidence backs it up,' said Sean. 'That's if you're prepared to accept the Bible as a factual, historical book.'

'Well, obviously I don't accept the Bible as a factual, historical book,' answered Roger. 'As you know, I regard most of it as a work of fiction.'

Sean paused for thought before coming back.

'If Jesus wasn't the Son of God, and if He didn't rise from the dead, why were His apostles prepared to die in defence of these truths? We've got evidence that all but one of His apostles were eventually put to death on the charge of spreading false beliefs. We actually have non-biblical, historical accounts of their executions. They were put to death for standing up for their faith and proclaiming Jesus to be God incarnate. Research in psychology tells us that no one ever dies for something they don't believe is true.'

While Roger and Paul mulled over his words, Sean continued to mount up more evidence.

'You can also look at biblical prophecy. The Old Testament is loaded with prophecies of the Messiah – the One who would save mankind. These prophecies foretold the life of Christ with astonishing accuracy. They predicted where and how He'd be born, how He would live, how He would die, what His legacy would be. They predicted all these things several hundred years before His birth. How do you explain that?'

'Easy,' said Roger. 'The people who wrote about Jesus' life twisted a few facts about Him to make it correspond with what was written in the Old Testament. So not in any way is that reliable evidence.'

Sean took a sip of his mineral water before coming back again.

'Okay, leaving the prophecies about Christ to one side, what about all the other biblical prophecies?'

'What about them?' Roger groaned.

'Well, let me give you some examples,' said Sean. 'It was foretold in the Bible that the Jews would lose their land and be dispersed throughout the world but that ultimately they would get their land and nationhood back. This came to pass. Also, Jesus Christ Himself predicted that the Church He established – the Catholic Church – would remain forever and that the dogmas of the faith would always remain intact and never be corrupted. The fact that the Catholic Church is still standing after 2,000 years of people trying to destroy it from both the inside and the outside is nothing short of a miracle. And let me give you another prophecy. The Book of Revelation chillingly predicted the eventual emergence of an anti-Christian, one-world government and one-world economic system. We seem to be moving steadily in that direction right now, as we speak.'

'All this doesn't mean a thing,' said Roger. 'Someone can make a case that half the predictions of Nostradamus have come to pass. But so much of what he said was ambiguous and open to interpretation. The same can be said for the Bible. Words and passages can be twisted and made to mean anything you want them to mean.'

Paul then added his opinions.

'What makes me question the credibility of the Bible is all the miracles that take place in it,' he said. 'There's page after page of miracles or supernatural things going on. There's miracles occurring on a daily basis during biblical times, yet we don't see any of that now in our modern day. Why did they occur then but not now? Surely, if God made room for more miracles to occur in this day and age, more people would believe in Him. In fact, everyone would believe.'

Sean shook his head.

'A person may see miracle after miracle and yet still not put their trust in God,' he contended. 'The Israelites whom Moses led out of Egypt witnessed all those astounding miracles, yet most of them still turned their back on God and fell into idolatry. You're also wrong to think that miracles don't occur in this day and age. I assure you they do. They occur all the time, all over the world, right now, in our era.'

Roger raised his eyebrows.

'I haven't seen too many lately,' he scoffed.

'That's because you haven't searched,' said Sean. 'But like I said yesterday, I've seen miracles and I've personally experienced one.'

'Experienced one?' said Paul. 'Oh, you mean your healing?'

'Aye,' said Sean.

Roger rolled his eyes, still refusing to accept that Sean was miraculously cured. Then he had some questions for Sean.

'You say that miracles are occurring worldwide all the time? Why do we not get to hear about them? Why are they never on the news or in the newspapers? Why is there never anything on TV about them? Oh, don't tell me, it's because the world and the media are run by neo-pagan liberals with an agenda against Christianity, right?'

'Aye, that's exactly right,' said Sean. 'Christians know about these miracles but the wider world doesn't know because they're hidden from them for the very reason you've pointed out. Like I said yesterday, I know of countless people being miraculously healed through the power of Christ. I myself was supernaturally brought back from the dead and healed after my car accident. And I would encourage you to study the miracles that took place at Fatima or Lourdes – which science cannot account for. I have personal experience of the healing power of the water from Lourdes.'

'Lords?' said Roger. 'Are you talking about the cricket ground?'

'He means Lourdes, the town in France,' Paul pointed out. 'You get this holy water from there. I know a bit about Lourdes and Fatima, having been brought up a Catholic.'

'Then I'm surprised to hear you say no miracles take place in the modern age,' said Sean. 'One of the most incredible miracles in history took place in 1917 in Fatima.'

'Fatima?' asked an oblivious Roger. 'Where on earth is that?'

Sean took a deep breath before explaining the miracle of Fatima. When coaxing non-believers to the faith, he always kept the miracle of Fatima in reserve – to be used as a last resort.

'Fatima is a small, rural town in Portugal,' he began to explain. 'In 1917, Mary, the Mother of Christ – or Our Lady, as we like to call her – appeared to three shepherd children in a series of visions, where she made pleas for the world to turn from sin and turn back to God. At the end of these visions she promised the children that God would send a great miracle to prove to the people that she really did appear to them and that her messages were true. In October 1917 some 70,000 or so people in Fatima witnessed the miracle of the sun "dancing" in the sky.'

Roger was briefly silent.

'What?' he said.

'Aye, you heard me right,' said Sean. '70,000 people saw the sun dance in the sky, moving from right to left and left to right, and as it did so the colour of the sky turned into each colour of the rainbow – red, then orange, then yellow, then green, and so forth.'

Roger stared at Sean with indented eyebrows and an open mouth, so Sean continued.

'After the sun had danced for about ten minutes, it began to fall to the earth. People screamed in terror as the sun came hurtling down on them – they thought it was the end of the world. Just when it looked like the sun was about to reach the earth and incinerate everyone, it retracted back into the sky again to its rightful place. In the immediate aftermath there were several miracle healings: the deaf could hear; the blind could see; cripples were able to throw away their crutches, etc.'

A predictably sceptical Roger shook his head.

'Are you sure about all this?' he asked.

'Aye, I'm sure,' Sean replied. 'We have 70,000 witnesses, and we have photographs to show how many people were there. But there's more. The people who witnessed this miracle were stood on a hill just outside the town of Fatima. Prior to the miracle taking place it had been lashing down with rain. People's clothes were soaked and the ground beneath them was completely soaked and muddy. But in the aftermath of the sun touching the earth, people's clothing immediately dried and the ground beneath them became instantly bone dry – yet no one was scorched or physically hurt. This proves that the sun really did come down to earth and it wasn't an optical illusion.'

Roger and Paul remained silent, trying to digest what they'd just been told. Being brought up a Catholic, Paul vaguely knew of the miracle of Fatima, but no one had really explained it to him in detail. Sean then continued to speak.

'It should be pointed out that during the time of the miracle, Portugal was under the control of an aggressively secularist government, hell-bent on the destruction of the Catholic Church. So, more important than the physical cures that took place were the spiritual awakenings and conversions that came about as a result of this miracle. People who were passionately atheist or against the Church converted or reconverted back to the faith. Journalists from newspapers known to be anti-Catholic were compelled to report the miraculous events, and Fatima became a pilgrimage site for Catholics from all over the world.'

Roger stared into space and shook his head.

'There's got to be some sort of rational explanation for this,' he insisted. 'It must have been some sort of hoax or put-up job.'

'How?' said Sean. 'Okay, maybe if just a few people had seen it we could hold some suspicions, but at least 70,000 – probably more – witnessed it. Could that many people have been fooled?'

18

Sowing to the Spirit

The three of them continued to sit and drink inside The Saint George. While nursing their pints, Roger and Paul tried to pick the bones out of the miracle of Fatima. Paul put forward an idea.

'I wonder if the miracle could have been caused by some sort of mass hypnosis. The people were made to believe this all happened through some sort of hypnotic suggestion. Skilled hypnotists can do incredible things.'

'70,000 hypnotised at the same time?' Sean queried. 'That would be a pretty miraculous feat in itself!'

'Well, maybe it was just a natural solar phenomenon,' Paul then suggested. 'And people ended up exaggerating the truth and making it out to be bigger and better than it actually was?'

'If it was a natural solar phenomenon why didn't the whole world see it?' Sean argued. 'And people who witnessed it found it impossible to explain or make others comprehend how incredible and awesome this event was. They weren't able to exaggerate the truth even if they tried. Besides, how do you also explain the instant drying of the earth and the miracle cures?'

'Like I said yesterday, when people expect to be cured they've got more chance of being cured,' said Roger. 'You can't underestimate the power of the mind.'

Sean cracked a smile.

'All these explanations people give seem more implausible than the miracle itself,' he asserted. 'Why not accept that an incredible miracle took place in relatively modern times? If you found this miracle in the Bible you'd find it far-fetched and unbelievable. This is a miracle that ranks alongside the parting of the Red Sea in its magnificence, and yet it occurred in 1917 and we have emphatic evidence to support it.'

'Why is this miracle not common knowledge?' asked Paul. 'Why do so few people, apart from Catholics, know about it?'

'I know,' said Roger. 'Let me guess. It's cos the world and its media are in the control of secular liberals who are driven to stamp out Christianity and biblical morals. Is that right, Sean?'

'You're being sarcastic, but you're pretty much correct in what you say,' answered Sean. 'We've got a miracle that ranks alongside most you've read about in the Bible, and yet the secular world chooses to ignore it and sweep it under the carpet.'

While Roger and Paul quietly sipped their drinks, taking it all in, Sean felt the need to say more on the topic.

'Whilst the miracle was incredible, it was not the most important thing. More important were Our Lady's messages. The miracle took place so that people would take her messages seriously. As I said, her messages sought to bring people back to God and to turn from sin. In her messages were several prophecies. The apparitions took place in 1917 whilst World War I was taking place, and she promised that this war would soon end – which it did the following year. But she warned that a future, more terrible, war – which turned out to be World War II – would come if people didn't mend their ways, and she said God would send the world a sign to warn people of this coming war. In January 1938, a strange red light in the sky could be seen all across Europe, including Britain – this was the sign that signified that war was on the horizon, though scientists tried to pass it off as a natural phenomenon. We've subsequently learned that January 1938 was actually the month Hitler drew up plans for his invasion of Austria, and the rest is history. But there was another prophecy which is most significant for our current era. Our Lady gave warning of Russia "spreading her errors throughout the world". She made this prophecy whilst the Russian Revolution was taking place, and again this prophecy came to pass – and we're now living in the midst of it. Russia did spread her errors throughout the world, and all the errors of Russia emanate from atheist materialism – which denies God, denies the spiritual or supernatural, denies absolute truth and elevates the *state* to the position of God.'

'You're scaring me with all this prophecy stuff,' said Paul.

'But Our Lady gave humanity a solution,' said Sean. 'Her message sought to bring people back to God, and central to this was a request for prayer and sacrifice. She asked for a devotion to a prayer called the rosary, which is a prayer that meditates on the life and virtues of Christ. She also called us all to a life of sacrifice, asking us to be prepared to suffer for the good of others. We have to love until it hurts. Our Lady said we must humbly accept our sufferings and unite them to the redemptive suffering of Jesus. If we want to be a true follower of Christ we must be prepared to take up the cross and go through whatever sacrifices God calls us to, for the benefit of others. This goes completely against the modern world view which says that all that counts in life is pleasure, pleasure, pleasure, and we should avoid suffering at all costs.'

'So, you've admitted that Christianity is an anti-pleasure religion,' Roger contended.

'No,' said Sean, 'it's not an anti-pleasure religion. It's a religion that deals in truth. The truth is that we're living in a broken world, full of people in need. We can't ignore that reality. If we have aspirations to be good, loving human beings we cannot turn a blind eye to the needs of others. When I talk about people in need, I'm not just talking about the poor, or people with disabilities or illnesses. More important to consider are people in need of being saved. This world is full of people in need of salvation, of being brought to Christ.'

'Otherwise they'll end up in the burning fires of hell, right?' said Roger, derisively.

'You're mocking... but you're right,' said Sean. 'In the months leading up to the miracle in Fatima, Our Lady visited the three shepherd children on five separate occasions. On one of her visits she showed the children a terrifying vision of hell. The vision put the children in a state of terror, prompting Our Lady to mercifully stop it. But she needed to show them what happens to unrepentant sinners when they die. She told them that souls drop into hell like snowflakes, and the most common cause of people ending up in hell is sins against the flesh. Now, she said this in 1917 when you would think the world was a far more innocent and moral place. But if sins against the flesh were a problem in 1917, how big a problem must they be now in this debauched era? Sexual sin may not be the most serious sin – there are worse sins – but it is the most common sin, the most common reason why so many end up in hell.'

Sean then soberly looked at Roger as he spoke.

'This is why I have to warn you about what you're planning to do tonight,' he told him. 'I don't want to sound overdramatic, but the wrath of God will be upon you. There will be repercussions for your actions.'

Roger looked away, shaking his head.

'Don't try and scare me out of it,' he replied in defiance. 'I refuse to buckle under superstitious fears. I'm visiting that brothel tonight, and no fears of divine retribution are gonna stop me. I mean, what exactly is gonna happen to me? Am I gonna be struck down by lightning bolts from heaven as soon as I've carried out the wicked deed?'

'You'll be sowing rotten seeds, which will then beget rotten consequences for you,' Sean warned. 'This was at the heart of Our Lady's messages at Fatima – that there are serious consequences to sin.'

'Well, that's a chance I'm prepared to take,' a still-defiant Roger replied. 'I've been looking forward to it all day, and I'm afraid there's no way I'm pulling out of it now. Your God will just have to forgive me.'

'As I said before, break God's Commandments and they'll break you,' Sean restated. 'You might not pay the consequences right away, but you will pay, sooner or later. All bad actions plant bad seeds, and we will always eventually reap what we sow.'

Roger contemptuously smiled at these words of warning, but that didn't put Sean off.

'All of our actions have consequences,' Sean continued. 'Good actions, even if they bring some initial suffering, will always result in good consequences in the end. Bad actions, such as looking at pornography magazines or, even worse, having your way with a prostitute, although providing some short-lived pleasure, will bring you harm in the long term. Whenever we do good, we sow good seeds and will reap a good harvest. When we do evil, we put down rotten seeds which will eventually bring forth rotten crops. That's why it always pays to sow to the spirit and not the flesh.'

'Leaving aside all this needless talk of seeds and sowing, what you're basically saying is that good will always come to good people and bad will always come to bad people, right?' said Roger.

'Aye,' said Sean, 'that's the hook and crook of it.'

'Well, what you say just doesn't correspond with what happens in the real world,' Roger put forward. 'This world is full of crooked people who do terrible things and no comeuppance comes their way; nothing bad happens to them. You've got gangsters and criminals who live in luxury mansions and drive fancy cars and live the life of Riley. They've got money, power and privileges on tap. For them, being bad and being sinful pays.'

Sean shook his head.

'They might have an abundance of privileges, but I promise you they live in a world of darkness and emptiness,' he replied. 'If they die without repentance of their sins they'll only end up in one place. Y'see, when I talk about something bad happening to an unrighteous person, I'm speaking in the context of harm being done to their soul. Let me give you an example... A person might abuse their own sexuality by buying a pornographic magazine, and he might get some fleeting pleasure out of it, but once the pleasure goes away the pain will start because by committing this sin he has cut himself off from God. The more we are separated from God, the less grace we can receive. As I said earlier, we cannot experience true, long-lasting joy without God's grace. That's why people who are trapped in sin and separated from God devote themselves to anything that gives them pleasure – whether it's sex, drugs, food, money, power, whatever. These things become their idols because they're the only things that temporarily lift them out of their empty, discontented lives. The more dependent on their idols they become, the more they become separated from God, and that further fuels their idolatry. So they end up caught in their own vicious circle.'

There was silence, with Roger and Paul reflecting on Sean's words. Then Paul had a question.

'How does a person get out of this vicious circle?'

Sean smiled. He detected in Paul a desire to want to change.

'You have to start sowing to the spirit at the expense of the flesh,' he began to answer. 'For example, if you were to make a decision tonight to stop yourself from visiting sex shops; even though it would be hard for you and would cause you some discomfort to resist it, you'd be sowing to the spirit and setting down good seeds. Although you'd experience short-term suffering, you'd receive long-term gain. But you would have to beg God for the grace to overcome all temptations because you wouldn't manage it by your own strength. But the good news is, the more you resist temptation and sow to the spirit, the stronger you get and the easier it gets. And if you're really serious about overcoming sin in your life, you need to go back to your Catholic faith and go back to Confession – that would clean you up, get the devil out, and get you right with God, and you would receive an inflowing of sanctifying grace, putting you in a much stronger position to fight temptation.'

Sean then delved into his pocket and brought out a holy picture card displaying an image of Christ on the cross, with the words "Passion of Christ, Strengthen Me" printed on it.

'Here,' said Sean, handing the card to Paul. 'Take this and look at it during times of temptation. It might help. I had it blessed by a priest.'

Paul, though, was reluctant to take it.

'No, you keep it,' he insisted, pushing it back in Sean's direction. 'It's not for me. I'm not religious.'

'Well, keep it anyway, in case in the future you change your mind,' Sean said.

Paul was still reluctant to take it. He didn't fancy going around the red-light area with this holy item in his pocket. But out of courtesy he felt he had to accept.

'Okay, thanks,' he said, putting it in his pocket.

Sean then turned to Roger again to speak.

'I'll say to you again, all our actions have a consequence for us. It's all part of the natural, universal law ordained by God. Whether you like it or not, or whether you know it or not, you will reap whatever you sow.'

Sean then took a coin out of his pocket to demonstrate a point.

'The principle of reaping what you sow is every bit a part of the natural, universal law as the law of gravity,' he said, dropping the coin down from one hand to the other to make the point. 'I'm demonstrating the law of gravity with this coin. Whatever action you take in life, either good or bad, will have a consequence, either good or bad. The law of sowing and reaping works just as decisively and consistently as the law of gravity. It is impossible to sin and get away with it, just as it would be impossible for this coin to stay up in the air when I let go of it. D'you see what I'm trying to get across?'

'I think you're labouring the point, but I can see what you're getting at,' said Roger. 'I know what you're saying, but I'm afraid I still don't agree. Sorry.'

Sean remained silent. He felt he'd said all that needed to be said. He couldn't force his ideas and beliefs on Roger, only present them to him in love and charity.

Eventually, the three of them left The Saint George, with Sean going his own way for the remainder of the night.

19

The Last Night of Vice?

After leaving The Saint George and parting company with Sean for the rest of the night, Roger and Paul headed back to the red-light area. They were now back inside Steenkamp's Coffee House, smoking joints. Roger felt the need to smoke to calm his excitement before his visit to the Dutch blonde. It seemed that Sean's words hadn't put him off going ahead with it. Meanwhile, Paul was in two minds as to whether or not to try and talk Roger out of it. He wouldn't admit it, but he'd been affected by all the religious talk from Sean.

'Ss-o, you're still keen to go thh-rough with it tonight?' said Paul to Roger, slurring his words.

'I shh-ure am,' said Roger, equally slurring. 'I just

need to ssh-moke more of this to cool my nerves, thh-en I'll be off to see her.'

Paul observed the dopey, glazed eyes of Roger. Even though he was pretty stoned himself, he was still able to recognise the same symptoms in his friend.

'Are… are you shh-ure you'll be in a fit enough ss-tate?' he asked.

'Yes,' said Roger, 'I'll be in a ff-it enough state; don't you worry about thh-at.'

'And you're not worried about what Sean said about breaking God's laws and ss-owing bad seeds ff-or yourself?' Paul warned Roger.

'Don't get ss-tarted with all that ss-owing bad seeds cobblers!' Roger retorted.

Paul inhaled some of his joint before speaking again.

'What about all thh-e evidence he mounted up to back up his faith, especially thh-ose miracles he talked about? Doesn't it make you think?'

'No,' answered Roger. 'All thh-e evidence he gave was questionable and could be argued with. Those ss-upposed miracles he described must have rational explanations behind thh-em. Just because thh-ey haven't found any rr-ational explanations yet doesn't mean there aren't any.'

Roger then gave Paul a sinister look before firing an accusation.

'I ss-ee Sean's ss-lowly but surely brainwashing you with all his rr-eligious codswallop.'

Paul shook his head.

'No he's not,' he answered. 'Like I ss-aid before, I like to keep my mind open to the truth.'

'Truth?' said Roger, shaking his head. 'Thh-ere's no such thing as truth.'

Paul took another drag of his joint.

'According to Sean, Jesus is thh-e Truth,' he then replied. 'And who can say whether he's rr-ight or not?'

Roger remained silent, deciding not to respond.

'I'm thh-inking of putting it to the test,' Paul then announced.

'Putting what to thh-e test?' asked Roger.

'Christianity,' said Paul.

Dopey Roger said nothing. He just glared at Paul with an open mouth.

'I'm thh-inking of putting it to the test ff-or six months to ss-ee if it will do me any good,' Paul continued. 'I want what Sean has. I want his ss-trength and confidence. I want to know what it's like to get by in life without booze, drugs and porn and yet still ss-eem so together and happy like he is.'

'Rr-ight, I'm off,' said Roger, stubbing his joint out. 'Having one Jesus ff-reak to contend with is bad enough; now I'll have to start coping with another one!'

Roger then got up to leave. He was ready to head over to the brothel.

'I'll ss-ee you in an hour's time in The Saint George,' he told Paul before walking out.

Paul was then left to smoke on his own, left pondering on what Roger was about to get up to. Was

Roger right in his assertion that he was merely indulging in some harmless fun with another consenting adult, or was Sean right – that Roger was committing a deeply sinful act in defiance of God's natural moral law?

Time passed and Paul remained sitting and smoking on his own in Steenkamp's Coffee House. Even in his semi-sedated state he was feeling a mixture of intrigue and unease over Roger's visit to the prostitute, wondering how it would go and whether he should have tried harder to talk him out of it. A part of him even felt a little repulsed over what Roger was doing, and he was increasingly feeling a sense of shame over his own dissolute way of life.

While he continued to puff on his joint, Paul imagined what life would be like, and what *he* would be like, if he had no vices. The thought of not having any attachment to any vice was an extremely attractive one. There was something pure, even manly, about a man with the strength to say no to life's temptations. And he considered the differences between people who heavily indulged themselves in vice and those who lived cleanly. There was no doubt in his mind that people who led clean, moderate lives tended to be stronger, more together and appeared to be happier.

Paul could sense a yearning deep within himself to get clean. There was a growing awareness that there was something wrong with the lifestyle he was leading. He had lost the innocence and purity of his

Catholic upbringing, and something inside of him was craving to get it back. He meditated on the seemingly clean and wholesome ways of Sean. A part of him felt envious towards Sean, envious of his inward strength and restraint. On top of that, Sean's words had had a definite effect on Paul, frightening him a little and giving him something to think about – especially in regards to what Sean had said about the consequences of deliberately leading a life of sin.

In the midst of his smoking, various thoughts and questions began to circulate around Paul's head. He pondered, *What if Sean's right? What if the Christian way is the right way? What if the current way I'm living my life is leading me down a path to ruin, a path to damnation even?* He then began to consider more deeply experimenting with Christianity for six months, putting it to the test to see if it would do him any good. While he puffed on his joint, he considered giving up weed and cutting down on alcohol. He considered removing pornography from his life and, following that, making an attempt to overcome all sexual self-indulgence. He knew deep down that all these vices he was attached to – for all the short-lived pleasure they provided – were hindering him in the long term. They were stopping him from being the best he could be. He knew he could never fulfil his potential or make the most of himself while these vices continued to have a grip on him.

As Paul continued to puff away on his joint, he was hit by a light of inspiration – perhaps divine inspiration

– and he made a sudden decision that this would be his final night of vice. After this night, he would make a conscious effort to abstain from all these vices and start again as a new man. He knew that if he could overcome all his vices, the sky would be the limit. The way would be paved open for him to achieve all his goals, and nothing would be beyond him. If he could live a clean, wholesome life, surely all his endeavours and pursuits would receive God's blessing, and he could become the man he was born to be!

As Paul was approaching the end of his joint he decided he'd smoke another one and then head out and explore the sex shops again before meeting back up with Roger at The Saint George. If this was to be his final night of vice he felt he had to make the most of it. After this night would come a new beginning, and he was excitedly looking forward to a new, brighter tomorrow. And while dreaming of making his dreams come true, he stared at the joint he was smoking and a thought came into his head – *The first thing I must do to make my dreams come true is stop smoking these!*

At around 11pm Paul left Steenkamp's and headed right into the heart of the red-light district. After all the walking around he'd done with Roger, he was now quite familiar with the area and was confident to walk around on his own. He was walking along the Oudezijds Voorburgwal canal, again exploring the X-rated shops. This activity would soon be consigned to his past, so he felt he had to make the very most of going in and out of these various stores to magazine-browse.

Paul found a shop he'd visited earlier with Roger. He recognised it from the large, bright, purple signboard above the shop window. The shop was called Jan's House of Pleasure, and it was situated at the beginning of a side street off the Oudezijds Voorburgwal canal. It was a shop where people were usually left alone to browse without being hassled by any counter assistant and this encouraged Paul to walk in. As well as magazines, the shop also had a selection of videos, along with three video booths (where customers could pay to watch a film right there and then). Once inside, Paul spent time going through as many magazines as he could, being selective by targeting the ones with the prettiest cover girls. Before leaving the shop he had a quick scan of the videos in spite of the fact he was soon due to meet back up with Roger at The Saint George and wouldn't have time to watch anything. One video caught his eye, prompting him to pick it off the shelf. On the front cover was a very pretty lady with jet black hair, beguiling blue eyes and an attractive, toothy smile that had Paul captivated. Paul then looked at the back cover details and found that the lady in question was an American porn actress by the name of Jemma Lee Jones – and she had managed to transfix him by her beauty.

Without putting up much of a fight, Paul caved in to his impulses. The visual stimulation dictated that he had to watch this film. He was desperate to watch it but was due to meet Roger at The Saint George and thus had no time to. *But I just have to watch this film!* Certainly, he had to watch it before leaving Amsterdam, though after this night he would only have half a day of his holiday left. He asked the shopkeeper if the store was open for business as usual on Sundays and was told that it was (not that a porno outlet was likely to respect the holiness of Sundays). He told the man behind the counter that he'd be in the following afternoon to watch the film. His planned new life of abstinence would just have to wait another day. After all, what would it matter if his new life of purity got started on Monday when he was back at home? And what better way to finally sign off from a lifestyle of decadence than by watching this film? And taking into account his pledge to lead a cleaner life, surely the Lord Almighty would be charitable and turn a blind eye to this final bit of sinning... wouldn't He?

20

The Morning After

It was Sunday morning – the morning after the night before. Roger was on his own, eating breakfast in the dining room of his hotel. While Paul was still tucked up in bed, Roger had barely managed a couple of hours of sleep. He'd been hit by insomnia despite the late night and all the drinking and dope-smoking that had gone on. An unpleasant episode of the previous night had had the effect of impeding some much-needed sleep.

Roger appeared a sad, crestfallen figure as he poked his knife and fork into his plate of bacon, sausage and eggs. His "date" the night before with the beautiful Dutch blonde had ended up an embarrassing disaster. A mixture of too much alcohol, too much Thai grass and an inability to relax had left him impotent and incapable. Never in his life had his manly pride and dignity taken such a hammering. He'd received little patience, understanding or sympathy from the prostitute, who was only interested in the colour of his money and in what *he* could do for *her*. He'd paid her for twenty minutes but had barely got ten. So not only was he humiliated, he'd also been soundly ripped off. Later, he'd met up with Paul at The Saint George but told him nothing of what had really happened. He'd put on a false front and made out that it had all gone really well.

So, now Roger was right down in the depths of desolation, and nothing could take these miserable, stomach-churning feelings away – not even the comfort food of bacon, sausage and eggs. While he got his head down into his grub he didn't notice someone approach.

'Morning, Roger,' he was greeted.

Roger lifted his head. It was none other than a very smartly dressed Sean, who had just attended early morning Mass at the nearby St Nicolaas Basilica and was in his best double-breasted suit. On seeing who it was, Roger broke into a half smile. In his depressed, lonely state he was actually quite pleased to see Sean's friendly face.

'Morning,' Roger replied. 'You're looking a bit smart this morning.'

'I've just attended an early morning Mass at the basilica,' Sean told him. 'I try not to eat anything before receiving Holy Communion, but I'm ready to eat now so I think I'll join you. Anyway, I'm surprised to see you down this early. I'd have thought you'd still be snoozing in bed after your late night.'

'I… I struggled to sleep last night,' revealed Roger.

'Really?' said Sean. 'Are you okay?'

'I'm okay,' claimed Roger. 'I'm just a bit down.'

'Oh dear,' said Sean.

Sean noticed the desolation in Roger's eyes, and it didn't take much for him to work out that the previous night hadn't gone well. He was dying to know the full details of what had happened, but he didn't want to get too nosey or personal.

'Well, I'll just grab something to eat and then we can talk about it, if you want,' he told Roger, who gave no response.

Sean went over to the breakfast serving table and took some bacon and eggs for himself before taking a seat opposite Roger. They both sat eating in silence for a while before Roger decided to spill the beans on what had happened. Although the issue was very personal, he really wanted to share his woe with someone.

'Can you keep a secret?' he asked Sean.

'Of course,' Sean assured him.

'You might have gathered, last night didn't go too well,' Roger admitted. 'The drinking and dope-smoking took its toll on me. I wasn't in the right physical state to do anything. And that money-grabbing harlot I was with just wouldn't give me any time to get my act together.'

Sean remained silent. Secretly, he couldn't help but feel a little pleased that Roger's planned night of joy had gone pear-shaped. Any sympathy and compassion he had for Roger were drowned out by a feeling of contentment that it had all gone horribly wrong for him.

'Afterwards, I met up with Paul down the pub,' Roger continued. 'I tried to make out that it all went really well. I put on this false front, but I'm not sure whether he believed me or not. You won't tell him what I've just told you, will you?'

'No, of course not,' Sean reassured him.

'I think I can trust you,' said Roger. 'You're the only person I know who I could have confided in. Anyone else would have had a great laugh at my expense and taken real pleasure in my humiliation. But I don't think you're that way inclined.'

Sean, however, couldn't help but take some pleasure from it, though he was trying hard not to show it. Sean knew that Roger's visit to the prostitute hadn't just been driven by lust, it had also been driven by pride and ego. Having his wicked way with the best-looking prostitute in Amsterdam was something Roger had really wanted to brag about. Therefore, for Sean, the best thing that could have happened to Roger was this humiliation – as humiliation is always the best antidote to pride!

'Y'know, sometimes little humiliations can be good for the soul,' Sean then said to Roger.

Roger smiled wryly.

'It was more than just a "little" humiliation,' he responded. 'It was a major, major embarrassment. I don't think I'll ever get over it. I know you'll probably say that I got my comeuppance for breaking God's moral law, right?'

Sean remained quiet.

The two of them sat eating in silence for a while. In the midst of their silence, Sean pondered as to why all the things he'd said to Roger in the previous two days seemed to have no effect on him – in that he'd still carried on with his lewd activities and still visited the prostitute. Sean pondered as to why nothing seemed to get through to Roger, and he wondered why he was so closed off to Christianity. What was the obstacle, or obstacles, stopping Roger from being open to the truth?

'So, in all the conversations and debating we had, did nothing I said give you something to think about?' Sean asked.

Roger had a brief think.

'Not really,' he eventually replied. 'I'm still an agnostic.'

'But is there any reason why you're so closed off to Christianity?' Sean asked.

Roger paused for thought again.

'I can't believe in anything that we don't have concrete proof for,' he said. 'It's as simple as that.'

Sean wasn't buying this. He knew there were other, more prominent, reasons keeping Roger away from the faith – like his attachment to licentious living. He decided to dig a bit more.

'Is lack of proof the only reason,' he asked, 'or is there anything else?'

'What do you mean?' Roger questioned.

'Well,' said Sean, 'I suspect the main reason why most people reject the faith when it gets presented to them isn't due to lack of proof but rather due to idolatry.'

Roger was briefly silent.

'Idolatry?' he then queried.

'Aye,' said Sean. 'Giving your life to Christ means having to surrender certain things. As I said yesterday, the way of Christ is the way of sacrifice, and most people just don't want to lead sacrificial lives – they don't want give up pleasures or comforts for the sake of following Christ. They don't want the cross and they don't want to die to themselves.'

Much to his liking, Sean found that Roger was actually listening to him quite intently, without his usual smirking. He seemed a tad more humble and receptive this morning. However, Roger still had apprehensions about what Sean was telling him.

'You talk about "the way of the cross" and "dying to oneself", but that isn't a very attractive proposition,' said Roger. 'I mean, what exactly is the point of life if it revolves around suffering?'

'The way of the cross may seem like the harder way, but in fact it isn't,' Sean answered. 'Jesus said: "Learn from me, for I am meek and humble of heart, my yoke is easy and my burden is light." He wasn't saying through these words that Christians won't suffer. What He was saying was that a person who follows Him will be at peace. Though he may suffer, he will experience internal joy, a joy that comes with being in friendship with God. Y'see, suffering comes to everyone in this life because we're living in a broken world, corrupted by sin. But we have the choice to suffer with Christ or without Him. It is easier to suffer with Christ than without him – that's why the way of the cross is actually the less burdensome path. And you say you can't see any point to suffering in this life and we should avoid suffering at all costs, but that's because your focus is all on this world and not on the afterlife. Our life here on earth is but a preparation for eternity. We have to live for love of God and neighbour here on earth so that we can receive our eternal reward in heaven.'

'Sorry, Sean, but I can't take a chance on there being such a place as heaven… or hell, for that matter,' Roger replied.

'In that case I'll just have to keep praying for you, Roger,' said Sean, 'that one day you'll see the light and come to the faith. With prayer, anything and everything is possible.'

Roger defiantly shook his head.

'I wouldn't waste your energy,' he answered. 'It's never gonna happen. There's no way I'll ever attach myself to any religion.'

'Never say never, Roger,' Sean asserted. 'My prayers usually get answered, one way or the other.'

21

The Spirit Versus the Flesh

It was mid Sunday afternoon. While Roger and Sean were winding down in the hotel, Paul had wandered out on his own. He was walking along the Damrak, heading towards De Wallen one last time. In a few hours he'd be back on the plane home, but before that there was a final bit of vice he had to indulge himself in. With a spring in his step, he was heading in the direction of the red-light district to seek out Jan's House of Pleasure – the X-rated shop he'd walked into the night before. He just had to watch the contents of that video that had so powerfully caught his attention the previous night. He couldn't leave Amsterdam without watching the video featuring the stunning Jemma Lee Jones. Any inclinations he had to begin a new life of holiness and purity would have to be put on hold for at least another day. And if Roger had dared to visit a prostitute the night before, surely just watching a porn video was a minor transgression in comparison… wasn't it?

For a Sunday the streets felt fairly busy (tourists making up for the absence of business people). As usual there appeared to be lots of Brits about, and as Paul approached the side street that led to the red-light district he caught sight of the young English busker he'd come across on Friday. As on Friday, the young man was sitting on some flattened cardboard, strumming his acoustic guitar. As Paul reached the point where the busker was sitting, he refrained from giving him anything and just walked on by.

Paul then put his hands into his pockets to double check that he had enough money to watch the video. He had on the same trousers he'd worn the previous night, and as he pulled out some gilders from his pocket he accidentally brought out the holy picture card of Christ on the cross which Sean had given him the previous night. The sight of the holy card briefly startled Paul – it brought back memories of the previous night and Sean's words about the seriousness of sin and the consequences of sin… and how Christ died to put away sin! Paul quickly put the holy card in his back pocket and was even tempted to chuck it in the nearest bin. The sight of it had induced a little feeling of guilt about what he was about to do. As he walked he tried to put the image he'd just seen out of his head. He tried to convince himself that what he was about to do was nothing too serious. After all, what harm was he doing anyone in just privately watching a porn video?

However, as Paul walked towards the shop, he couldn't help but ponder on the consequences of doing what he was about to do, and this was just giving him second thoughts. But quickly after having these second thoughts, images of Jemma Lee Jones came racing back into his head, quashing any ideas he had about not watching it. The lure of this Jemma Lee Jones was too much, and God would just have to understand and forgive him.

Paul soon found himself on the Oudezijds Voorburgwal canal. As he walked along the canal, he spotted the start of the side street where Jan's House of Pleasure was located. From a distance he could see the bright, purple signboard. He walked along the right-hand side of the canal towards it, but as he walked these forewarning thoughts continued to pop into his head. He could feel something inside trying to warn him of the consequences of what he was about to do, and this made him slow up and hesitate. It was as though his conscience had suddenly decided to get to work on him and make him think twice about his intentions. What hit his mind was a vivid recollection of Sean's words explaining how it was impossible to sin and get away with it. Whether the sin was big or small, it would always be dealt with by God. And the deliberate committing of a sin would always have bad consequences, sometimes very bad consequences.

An apprehensive Paul began to walk very, very slowly towards the shop. The sudden fear of harsh repercussions was stifling his steps. When he left the hotel he'd had no hesitations about going to watch this film. The only thing dominating his mind then was the exciting prospect of seeing this Jemma Lee Jones in action and all the pleasure that would come with it. At the start of his journey he'd had few qualms about indulging in this final bit of pleasure-seeking – it was something his body and mind were compelling him to do. But it was in the aftermath of accidentally pulling out the holy card and seeing the image on it that a hesitancy was activated within him. There was this sudden fear that he'd be planting very bad seeds indeed by deliberately committing a sin he knew to be highly offensive to God.

Paul needed time to think. He decided to turn himself round and walk back up the canal again. He had to carefully weigh up the pros and cons of going in to watch this film. He checked his watch. He knew he didn't have much time and needed to be back at the hotel at least within the next two and a half hours or so.

The problem now for Paul was that although he knew deep down that watching this film would do him absolutely no good, his body just wasn't listening. From the moment he woken up this morning he'd been looking forward to watching this film, and there'd been such a build-up of anticipation inside him that literally his mouth was now watering in readiness for it. There was just too much excitement and enthusiasm tingling inside him to walk away. Therefore, before getting even halfway up the canal, he turned himself back around and started walking down towards the side street. With quick steps he walked in the direction of the shop with a resolve to go inside and watch the film and just get it out of the way.

With visions of Jemma Lee Jones circulating around his head, Paul walked onwards towards Jan's House of Pleasure. But as soon as he got in sight of the bright, purple signboard, something hit his mind, and he once again felt compelled to slow down and think again. The sight of the shop actually seemed to trigger an alarm in his mind, and he could sense an inner voice screaming in his head telling him: "*No!*" Something so strong inside was telling him that he had to resist, he had to fight this temptation. The inner voice was telling him that he had to win this battle against his own flesh, regardless of the discomfort and mental torture that would come with resisting it. If he caved in now he would cave in the next time, and the next time, and the next time. There was no such thing as tomorrow. He had to start breaking the shackles of this sin now.

By the time Paul reached the shop his resolve to watch the film had gone away again. He turned himself around and started walking back up the canal again, getting exasperated by his own indecisiveness.

As Paul walked, he decided to encourage himself not to watch the film. He reminded himself of Sean's explanation as to why pornography was so harmful. He reflected on how porn reduces people, most often women, to objects of lust. And it's lust that reduces a human being to a thing, an image, an object to be used for someone else's pleasure. Therefore, porn degrades and de-humanises a person.

Paul then encouraged himself to think more deeply about Jemma Lee Jones the human being, as opposed to Jemma Lee Jones the porn actress. He delved into his imagination and tried to conceive of her as a real person, a real human being with emotions and feelings and complexities like everyone else – someone who breathes, eats and sleeps; someone who thinks, laughs, cries and feels pain. She's someone's daughter, maybe someone's sister, maybe even someone's mother.

Paul then remembered being told how in America a chillingly high percentage of sex industry workers don't make it past the age of forty. They end up so psychologically messed up and disturbed that it pushes them into self-destruction – often by way of additional involvement in drugs. And could this Jemma Lee Jones be part of that statistic as one of those no longer living and breathing on the earth?

After these reflections, Paul made his mind up not to watch the film or give any more money to an industry that did so much harm. He'd finally seen the light... he thought. He turned left onto a side street out of the Oudezijds Voorburgwal canal and looked to head straight out of the red-light district.

Eventually, Paul got onto the side street that was a way out of De Wallen and he was soon in sight of central Amsterdam's high street, the Damrak. He walked steadily in that direction, moving away from the modern-day Sodom that was Amsterdam's red-light district. However, although he'd fully made up his mind that he was never going to get involved with porn ever again... both his body and his imagination still weren't listening! His body was still swamped with hormones, generated by the ongoing excitement and anticipation of watching the film. His head continued to be peppered by the image of Jemma Lee Jones, reminding him of how gorgeous she was and that he couldn't pass this opportunity of getting to see her in such a revealing way. In spite of all the self-persuading and all the good, moral reasons he gave himself to walk away from it, he still badly wanted to watch it. The curiosity inside him was just too intense. He just had to watch it.

Paul again turned around and headed back into the red-light area and onto the Oudezijds Voorburgwal canal. Yet again, he headed in the direction of the shop. It was no use. He just had to satisfy his curiosity and let this temptation get the better of him. But, predictably, as soon as he got within close proximity to the shop and the bright, purple signboard, his conscience was once again making him hesitate and slow down. This was now getting ridiculous! He checked his watch again, knowing that he couldn't continue to dilly-dally like this for much longer.

Why was it that as soon as he'd made up his mind not to watch the film, the appeal and attraction of it suddenly intensified again in his mind? Conversely, now that he'd made the decision to watch it, his guilty conscience had come back to the fore, warning him not to go through with it. It was as though a spiritual tug of war was taking place in his own mind, with an angel pulling him one way and a demon pulling him another.

Paul fully knew what the right thing to do was, but he didn't have the will or strength to do what he knew to be right. Then he remembered Sean's words, explaining how a person couldn't resist temptations by his own power. It was only by the grace of God that a person could fight them. Both the sinful nature and the devil were too powerful for any human being to fight on their own. With this in mind, Paul moved to seek divine help.

As Paul slowly walked down the canal in the direction of the shop, he made an attempt to pray. He kept his arms at his side and bowed his head as he silently and inwardly prayed an Our Father, and then he prayed in his own words: *Jesus, please help me. Please give me the strength to overcome this temptation.*

By the time Paul got to within a few yards of the shop he stopped and turned himself around to walk back up the canal again. He then kept inwardly repeating: *Jesus, please help me. Jesus, please help me. Jesus, please help me. Jesus, please help me.*

After continuously repeating these words, an idea came into his head. From his back pocket he again took out the holy picture card displaying the image of Christ on the cross, and he remembered Sean advising him to look at this image in times of temptation. He focused hard on the image. He saw the battered and bloodied body of Christ hanging on the cross and the words "Passion of Christ, Strengthen Me" above the image, and the sight of this greatly enlightened him.

By contemplating Christ on the cross, it eventually dawned on Paul that in order to overcome this temptation it was necessary to go through whatever discomfort and suffering was placed on him to achieve that end. He understood that he not only had to accept the suffering but also had to embrace it. He had to unite the suffering, however major or minor it was, to that of Christ. He had to see it as a necessary penance, a penance which was unavoidable. He also comprehended that whatever discomfort he would go through would be very minor compared to the pain that Jesus had endured – that Jesus had endured for him.

Paul walked swiftly until he was out of De Wallen and could again see the Damrak. With greater assertiveness he was going back to the hotel, and nothing was going to stop him, because now he was ready to embrace and see as necessary the suffering and discomfort that would come with this act of self-restraint. It was his willingness to embrace the suffering and discomfort that now made all the difference.

Paul walked along the street, with central Amsterdam's high street in close view, and he again came into view of the young English busker, still sitting and strumming his guitar. As Paul walked towards the busker, a flash of inspiration came into his head. He decided to give the busker a generous chunk of his money. By doing this he knew he wouldn't have enough money on him to watch the film, thus giving himself no option but to go back to the hotel.

Paul delved into his pocket, pulled out a twenty-gilder note and handed it to the busker.

'Oh, thank you,' said the surprised busker as he gratefully took the note. 'Are you sure you want to part with this much?'

Paul decided to truthfully tell the busker why he'd handed him the money.

'I was going to spend this money on a porn film, but I'm trying to kick the habit and become a Christian.'

The busker smiled and then warmly chuckled.

'I'll pray for you in your endeavour,' he told Paul in all warmth and sincerity. 'God bless you.'

Paul was lifted by these encouraging words. He walked away, feeling pleased with himself. He felt he'd finally won an important first battle, snatching victory from the jaws of defeat.